under
the
baseball
moon

under
the
baseball
moon

JOHN H. RITTER

PHILOMEL BOOKS

PHILOMEL BOOKS

A division of Penguin Young Readers Group. Published by The Penguin Group. Penguin Group (USA) Inc., 375 Hudson Street, New York, NY 10014, U.S.A. Penguin Group (Canada), 90 Eglinton Avenue East, Suite 700, Toronto, Ontario, Canada M4P 2Y3 (a division of Pearson Penguin Canada Inc.). Penguin Books Ltd, 80 Strand, London WC2R 0RL, England. Penguin Ireland, 25 St. Stephen's Green, Dublin 2, Ireland (a division of Penguin Books Ltd.). Penguin Group (Australia), 250 Camberwell Road, Camberwell, Victoria 3124, Australia (a division of Pearson Australia Group Pty Ltd). Penguin Books India Pvt Ltd, 11 Community Centre, Panchsheel Park, New Delhi–110 017, India. Penguin Group (NZ), Cnr Airborne and Rosedale Roads, Albany, Auckland 1310, New Zealand (a division of Pearson New Zealand Ltd). Penguin Books (South Africa) (Pty) Ltd, 24 Sturdee Avenue, Rosebank, Johannesburg 2196, South Africa. Penguin Books Ltd, Registered Offices: 80 Strand, London WC2R 0RL, England.

Published simultaneously in Canada. Printed in the United States of America. Design by Gina DiMassi. Text set in Concorde. Library of Congress Cataloging-in-Publication Data   Ritter, John H., 1951–   Under the baseball moon / John H. Ritter.   p. cm.   Summary: Andy and Glory, two fifteen-year-olds from Ocean Beach, California, pursue their respective dreams of becoming a famous musician and a professional softball player. [1. Softball–Fiction. 2. Trumpet–Fiction. 3. Musicians–Fiction. 4. Interpersonal relations–Fiction. 5. California–Fiction.] I. Title.   PZ7.R5148Und 2006   [Fic]–dc22   2005027183   ISBN 0-399-23623-6

1 3 5 7 9 10 8 6 4 2

First Impression

to jolie,
pitcher, jazz girl, lover of the sea,
who always gives to me
una poca de gracia.
with love,
papa

acknowledgments

My great thanks to Judy Blume, crazy dreamer and author extraordinaire, who supported me and this story, emotionally and financially, through the vital Society of Children's Book Writers and Illustrators Judy Blume Award grant for a contemporary novel-in-progress.

Also, deep appreciation to M. Jerry and Helen Weiss, scholars extraordinaire, who spurred me to frame the concept of this novel in short story form for their anthology *Big City Cool* (Persea Books, 2002), where it appeared under the title "Old School/FuChar Skool."

And finally, with loving appreciation to Keiller Middle School principal Patty Ladd; author and soul support Susan Vreeland; OBcean artist and dreamer Jennifer Churchill; expert teenagers Sammy and Ashley Churchill and their OB gang; writers *brillantes* Beth Brust, Jayne Haines, and Stacey Goldblatt; editor extraordinaire Michael Green; my heart on fire, Cheryl Ritter, and her magnificent sixth-graders, the Explorer Elementary Charter School Class of 2005.

Con mucho amor a todos,

Juan

base·ball moon

1: Any daytime moon which rises in the mid to late afternoon; typically two to four days before the full moon. **2:** A term dating back to the early days of professional baseball, when ball fields were built facing the east to keep the afternoon sun out of the batter's eyes; the baseball moon was the nearly full moon rising over the center field fence during an afternoon game in April. **3:** An April moon, rising in the mid-afternoon, heralding the new baseball season.

under
the
baseball
moon

ahoy, you crazy dreamers!

Welcome to the water's edge of North America. *Bienvenidos, amigos,* to the sandy edge of San Diego, where many years ago, wagon wheels of the Spanish Fathers cut across a Kumeyaay Indian migration trail and changed this land forever.

Here, the midnight ocean waves roll in below a majestic pier and break upon the shore like a herd of wild white horses running wither to wither. And here, storytellers sit the warm day long casting their tales and singing their songs to surfers, bikers, sailors, *artistas,* skateboarders, shop owners, *y turistas.*

Welcome to the sands of Ocean Beach, in the land of the baseball moon. Come with me and walk the streets of this magical, organical beachtown filled with soul, filled with the spirit of long-lost freedoms, and known simply as "OB."

So blow *las trompetas* from atop the pier and bang the drums like thunder. And let us begin the tale of a moonstruck trumpeter who crosses the path of a softball star, stirring up dreamers, jokers, players, and rogues, and forever changing the cosmos.

Ay, mis amigos. Vamos.

the epitome of cool

Everything that happened in those days after OB Juan finally cleaned out the little apartment above his seafood-taco bar and grill was something no one saw coming.

My parents didn't see it. The guys in my band never saw it. And this mellow-down-easy California beach-town sure didn't see the over-the-moon, star-tossed disarrangements that one simple act of cleanliness would bring.

I think I was the first.

My name is Andy Ramos, and I grew up a little star-tossed and over the moon myself. In fact, I grew up thinking that backstage hustlers and cocktail waitresses were twenty-four-hour daycare providers. You see, my mom was a singer in a band and she spent most nights rocking under red stage lights with my dad by her side, flaming up the fretboard of an electric guitar. So I spent the first few years of my life in the dank, low-lit backrooms of smoky nightclubs with high-stepping women in low-cut trimmings tucking me in at night and singing me to sleep.

I also grew up with every kind of jazz, rock, bebop,

and hip-hop thumping my bones and flooding my brain 24/7 and more.

"Old school music," I called it. "Been around since *sound*."

"That old school music, *mijo*," my grandpa would tell me, "is your musical roots. Cut off your roots, Andrés, and pretty soon you are nothing but a hollow tree." Then he'd point his golden trumpet at me. "And there is nothing worse than being a hollow tree. Because music, *mijo*, comes only from what's inside."

Well, someplace inside of me, I agreed. It's just that I wanted to create a sound that went beyond roots. I'm talking about climbing here, riding tree limbs in the wind, scaling treetops up to the rooftops and beyond. And for the last five years, I'd been trying to do just that, ever since Grandpa Ramos gave me this old trumpet he'd won in a poker game.

Day after day, whenever he was in town, Grandpa would spend hours showing me how to play, how to breathe, how to reach my highs and lows. He'd hold up that dented Yamaha and teach me how to get my "chops out front." And I'd sit there under his spell watching his fingertips dance away, tripping the valves, while his tight lips pushed a hip, mellow "sweetness" out of that trumpet's golden brass bell.

In my eyes, Grandpa Ramos was the epitome of cool. He was confident and comfortable around anyone, anywhere. How I wished I could be like him, and learn from him "what a musician needs to know." That I could travel the musical world like him. And how I wished he had not died. That his liver had not stopped delivering the sugar to his blood. Because I'm sure he would have known what to do about the mess I was in now.

I guess the roots of my trouble go way back to the time I got that trumpet. That's when I began to be treated like the weirdo joke-magnet of our fifth grade class. But it wasn't because of the trumpet or anything I ever did. It was all on account of a girl. Glory Martinez.

And it was pure guilt by association.

When I was little, my folks were good friends with Glory's mom, who worked as a dancer and cocktail waitress all over town. Some nights she danced at the neon glitz-clubs on Rosecrans and other nights she served drinks at a place where my parents played called OB Juan Quixote's—the coolest little blue plaster, palm-treed, indoor-outdoor fish-taco and beer bar you've ever seen. But she really wanted to be a singer. Her name was Marlina Martinez, and she had a killer voice that would fill the room and fall on you like a warm blanket.

Whenever my folks were playing at OB Juan's, my dad would ask Marlina to step onstage and sing a song or two. And even though I was only four or five, and even though she'd just tucked me in, I'd sneak out from the back to watch. And, man, she'd paint the room with her voice, low and soft or loud and brassy. When she finished, my dad would always say, "Let's hear it for Marlina Martinez!" Then after the applause, he'd add, "She's sure got a *nice* pair of lungs." Then he'd always wink, and the audience would always laugh.

Later on, Glory and her mom moved into a little place just a couple doors down from us. I don't remember her mom ever getting really drunk, but I know that sometimes my dad would take her with him to AA meetings. On those nights Glory would show up at our place dressed in goofy homemade costumes like a rainbow-colored butterfly or some intergalactic princess. That was bad enough, but she also liked to wear them to school. When we were little, it was no big deal, but by the fourth grade, it got to be really embarrassing, especially since our parents were good friends—and so everyone thought Glory and I were good friends, too.

We weren't. I barely tolerated that girl's existence, to put it mildly, and she was totally oblivious to the way I felt. That's because she was totally out there. I mean, in orbit. She talked to imaginary people and danced whenever she felt like it and got in trouble a lot.

By fifth grade, Glory had slipped into a sort of gothy phase and started dressing in all black. Sometimes teachers would call me over and want me to go talk to her, like when she started freaking out or something. Once, during PE, some girl tripped her, so Glory got mad and picked up the basketball, screeching like a demon, and ran away with it.

"You'll all burn!" she screamed at us, then spun around and heaved the ball over the fence. "Be gone, *diablos*, be gone!" She had a really strong arm.

"Andrés," Mrs. Melbourne said, in front of everyone. "Will you please go talk to her? Just try to calm her down and get her to come back."

"Why me?" She had no idea how hard it was.

Then the guys would start in. "Because she's your *girlfriend*, Andy-Dandy. Come on." "Yeah, Andrés, you're her knight in shining armor. She *needs* you." They'd follow that with a round of loud, slobbery kissing noises.

But Mrs. Melbourne always won. She'd give me her pursed-lip, dipped-head, I-need-your-help look, and say, "Andrés, please."

My face would turn hot, and while someone ran off to get the ball, I walked off to find Glory. But the only way I could get her to turn her broom around and fly on back was to softly sing a little song she once taught me.

> The Flower Queen is coming.
> Do not be afraid.
> The Flower Queen is coming.
> Atop a horse of jade.

I know. It was very weird.

By sixth grade, I was the school fool and my reputation was a joke. I had constant stomachaches because of her. I was always worried, knowing that the next call to save her or to explain her or to defend her could come at any time.

Then, that summer, the greatest thing happened. Glory's mom started drinking again, but this time she checked herself into a rehab clinic in Arizona and sent Glory to live with her grandparents in Tucson.

You don't know how glad I was to see her go. I was like, "Finally. Now, I can relax. I can really be myself."

But instead, I suffered for the next couple of years. I'd be walking down the hall at school, and out of nowhere somebody'd say, "Hey, Andy-Dandy, when's your girlfriend coming back?" Or, "Yeah, Little Boy Blue, you gonna blow your horn and get her to come home?"

It wasn't every day, but it was enough to prolong my weirdo rep.

And a rep is a lot like a tattoo. Easy to get, but a lot harder to get rid of.

So I did the only thing I could think of to lift my spirits. I played the trumpet. Every minute I could. Some nights I'd climb out my window and onto the roof of our old two-story house and blow like a chimney stack, straight up to the moon.

Sometimes I'd skateboard under the Sunset Cliffs Boulevard Bridge, near Robb Field, where the San Diego River empties into the ocean. I'd sit up on the riprap and play to the girders and water pipes above, letting the concrete echo rain down on me. Lines of cars would rumble by, just over my head, their tires drumming the metal bridge joints—*tha-dump, tha-dump*—giving me my beat, and I'd blow like a jazzman under a blue light, keeping it tight, keeping it raspy, maybe stir up a few tourists from Nebraska.

And what I loved most was pushing the edge—fusing together different sounds and styles, like Latin jazz, reggae, and rap.

"Cultural Fusion," I called it. Just like my neighborhood in OB, California.

I even learned to play one-handed while skateboarding at the same time, racing down the beach boardwalk or into town, blowing like some bugle boy on a calvary horse leading the charge. And I was—the Fusion Charge!

Before long, my old rep started to change. By the ninth grade, people really started to like what I was doing. And by the time OB Juan had cleaned up and rented out the little place above his bar and grill, I'd already started writing songs, started up a band, and was ready to follow in the footsteps of my Grandpa Ramos. And last week, the first week in June, I made a promise to me and to him. I vowed I would devote every day this summer to the mission of launching my musical career. This would be my "breakout summer."

So early today, I cruised outside and decided to skate my way past the soccer greens and softball diamonds at Robb Field and climb up on a pile of jagged granite boulders near Sk8 Park. Working on a new melody, working the improv room of my brain the entire time, I settled on top of a flat rock to scope out the skateboarders inside, ant-trailing around the walls. Particularly the guys in my band, Lil Lobo and Tran.

As great a drummer as Lil Lobo was, he was even better at skateboarding. I watched him nosegrab his board, sprint about ten feet, drop it, and jump on, skating for the low metal rail. He ollied up, grinding the whole pipe, slid off, and rolled on, carving his way along the curvy plaster walls. That was music to my eyes. I put the trumpet to my lips.

He shot up the concrete wall. I shot a riff at him. He caught air and spun. I blew another. Sixteen beats. Four-four time. I followed his moves around the park.

Then Tran, my guitar player, flew by. In real life Tran Loc Tien was a shy, skinny kid whose family moved here from Vietnam before he was born. But at Sk8 Park, he was fearless. Down the empty swimming pool walls and up he glided, spun 180, then dropped back down. Eight beats. Cool, sweet.

It was like I was painting them with music.

Whatever they did, I played along. Some riffs I was old school, some riffs I was new. I was Wynton Marsalis, but I could be Dizzy, too.

After a while, I needed a change, so I started rolling down the asphalt bike path that ran riverside. As usual, I stopped skating just past the tennis courts and walked across the grass toward my outdoor "echo chamber," which some people call the handball courts. I loved to play in there. The acoustics were great.

On such a warm June day, the sports complex was full of people, jogging, kicking soccer balls. A couple of girls raced by on blades, laughing and talking and nearly crashing into a little old man leaning on a cane. There was action everywhere.

Across the huge grassy field, it looked like a tournament was about to begin at two of the softball diamonds. Swarms of bare-legged girls buzzed all around, carrying sports bags and bats. Some wore pink-and-black jerseys. Others were dressed in glittery turquoise tank tops and silver shorts. I watched while one shimmering blue-and-gold team swept onto the field, hollering like party girls dancing around a fire ring at the beach, as they snapped the ball to each other.

I looked for something to play. One girl was pitching to her coach. On a nearby diamond, I noticed another girl taking batting practice all by herself. Dressed in a sleeveless workout top, she was standing in the batter's box hitting orange plastic balls that were being shot out of a small machine. That looked interesting. I walked to the handball court closest to the field she was in, slid my back down the side wall until I was sitting on the concrete, and watched.

Every few seconds the batting machine sent out another ball.

The girl would stand in the batter's box and hit about a dozen balls or so—not too far—then walk out and load them all up into a wire basket that she took back and hung just above the machine. After that, she did it all over again.

This was something new, so I painted her. I played her loopy swing, the bounce in her knees, her slo-mo practice cuts. Even the sway of her dark ponytail. Took me no time at all to get into the rhythm of this tall, sweet athlete. The machine kept popping, she stepped and swung. I played away.

It was all free-form, improv, it was like dance jazz. I liked the way it sounded, so I played a little louder.

It took her a while to notice me. Not me really, but my riffles of sound. I saw her stop, then start again, to see if I was really doing what I was doing. And I stayed right with her.

She lowered her bat and looked over her shoulder.

"Hey!" she shouted. Her tone said it all. Playful, not serious. "What are you doing?"

I pushed myself up off the green concrete slab and

stepped out into the sunlight. With one eye squinted shut, I shrugged. "I'm working on my improv. Won't do it, if it bothers you."

She laughed and waved her hand, as if saying *It doesn't bother me.* I grinned at that.

She set up to hit again. I kept playing. With each swing, she smacked little bullet line drives that went about fifty feet, then died before they reached the outfield grass.

I studied her long legs, the whirl and whisk of her hair as she swung, the curl of her body, then the fury of her cut. My music fit her dance perfectly. And soon I became aware that I was playing sounds I had never heard before. It must've been the echo. This almost ghostly sound began to emerge, traveling like the distant treetop warble of a mockingbird calling in the night. It was just as unpredictable, too. I was playing as if my fingers were separate from my brain. And I realized she was the first girl I had ever painted.

After a while, a friend of hers—blond hair, not as tall—showed up holding two bottles of a purple sports drink. Next thing I knew, Tran was calling to me. He and Lil Lobo must've followed the sound of my horn.

"Hey, man," said Tran. "Pizza time. Come on."

I stood up and saw Lil Lobo already skating off toward Casanova's. I said nothing about the girl, just flipped my board up and left. But as I hit the sidewalk, a certain ping of panic hit me. What if I never see her again? I took one more look back. And I stopped. *I could not leave.*

"Tran!" I called out. "I'll meet you guys there."

I stood a moment in the warm sunlight, wondering what impulse I was listening to.

Grandpa? *¿Abuelito?* Is that you?

No answer.

Okay, I told myself, it's no big deal. I'll just stroll up, say hi, introduce myself. Don't want to bug her. Just scope her out, be like Grandpa, the epitome of cool, and then leave.

Taking in a huge breath, I strode forth. But as I got closer, the epitome of a jellyfish started swimming in the pit of me. I stepped through the gate and onto the ball field grass. She waved. I could not believe it.

No matter how long she'd been gone, how much she'd grown, I could still tell. It was Glory Martinez.

getting all ha-cha-cha

"**H**ey!" she said, and started walking my way.

Glory Martinez, I kept telling myself. *This* was the girl with the furious swing? The legs of steel? And—I soon noticed—her mom's sweet curves? The same girl I grew up referring to as my "stomachache waiting to happen"?

"Andy!" she called, actually jumping as she said my name and bouncing her necklace full of seashells. "I knew that was you. Play your trumpet again, okay? I love it. Makes me hit so much better."

She just started talking, like no big deal, like it had only been three minutes instead of three years.

Dude, I thought, you just played your heart out, getting all *ha-cha-cha,* over her? An intergalactic broom-rider?

I glanced at the row of trees off to my left. I wanted to turn, to run to them, but I was already so close. Her friend was staring at me, too.

"Oh," added Glory, pointing. "This is Kayla. I'm going to be trying out for her softball team in a few days. Kayla, Andy."

Kayla smiled. She was a pixie—freckled cheeks, short blond hair, bouncy, athletic. Maybe even normal. I started to feel better.

"Hi, Andy," she said. "I know you. I mean, I've seen you around before."

I nodded, though I wasn't sure I recognized her. She looked younger, maybe an eighth or ninth grader, and talked through a wide smile. "Glory says you play 'enchanting' music."

I raised a shoulder. "I guess." I bounced the trumpet against my leg, feeling an awful lot like the tongue-tied school fool all over again.

"He does," said Glory. "Andy, I love baseball now. Seriously. In Arizona, my grandparents took me to all of the Cactus League spring training games. So now I'm this huge fan. I've been playing softball like crazy, and now my big dream is to make the U.S. National team as a pitcher and go to the Olympics."

I peered at her. The Olympics? Playing softball? Like crazy? Well, that part made sense. Crazy was her specialty. "That's cool."

"Well, first I *have* to make Kayla's travelball team. That's why we're here. And I knew something *extraordinaire* was going to happen today."

"Why?" I still couldn't believe I was talking to her.

"Because there's a baseball moon."

"A what?" I asked.

"A baseball moon. You know." She whirled and

pointed at the round, white cloud of a moon just above the hills to the east. "There, see it?"

"Why do they call it that?"

"Well, because back before they had lights, they'd play baseball in the afternoon. And sometimes people saw the moon rise up at the start of a game, so they started calling it 'the baseball moon.' " She shrugged. "That's what I always heard, anyways. And my grandfather says I play so well because I was born in August, under a baseball moon."

"That's a cool story," said Kayla. "I never knew any of that."

I hadn't either, but I only nodded, fully noticing that, no doubt, Glory was an athlete now. Her pudgy face was leaner, her arm and leg muscles stronger, more defined. And she was as tall as I was, at least five ten or something. I could hardly believe I was looking at the same girl. "So, you're back? I mean, you're living here now?"

She hummed and nodded, then smacked her lips. "Yup. Me and Mom. Just moved back. We've got this cute little apartment on top of OB Juan Quixote's. We were all set to move to Los Angeles, but Mom just had to stop in OB on the way. And OB Juan was just finishing up painting the place, and *ta-da*! Here we are."

I nodded again. "Yeah, that's cool."

"And don't worry, I know OB Juan's serves alcohol, but Mom's all sober now. She's into computers and

Glory leaned over to pick up a ball by

Speaking of her mom. Those smooth, round,
ite half shells hanging from her necklace
s she dipped, clacking together just like the
nd silver necklaces her mom always wore—a
sound I hadn't heard, or thought about,

ly, she rose. "You still live at the same place?
l house on Niagara?"
h." Man, I needed to leave, but she was being

u play really well, you know that? Are you
o play professionally, in clubs and stuff, like your
nd dad?"
m, yeah—hope so." Although my whole plan was
o get stuck here in Ocean Beach playing
clubs.
Play some more, okay?" she asked. "Show Kayla
you were doing."
gave them both a look and then decided that, ac-
ly, it would be a relief to sink into some music, to
e behind my horn. It would definitely help my
athing. "Okay."
Glory ran back to the batter's box. Kayla started
e machine.
I moved toward the dugout, so I wouldn't be too
ose to her or too loud. At first, I just watched and let

the machine set the tempo. After a few pitches, I started to relax. On the next pitch, I strode in with a quick riff, something I hoped to build a melody on. Glory giggled and swung.

In a while, I spotted four things she always did while she got ready to hit. First, she rested the bat on her right shoulder, then she yanked it up and back. When the ball appeared, she took a small step forward with her front foot. Finally, she launched her swing. Before long, I could play all four motions. Rest, ready, step, swing. Rest, ready, step, swing.

I looked even closer, studying her for tiny things. Like how her slender fingers, in their black leather gloves, squeezed the bat really hard right before each swing, how she lifted the heel of her front foot first, before she stepped, how the muscles in her upper arms expanded before they would explode.

Sometimes—like when she kicked the dirt after a pop-up—I saw the wild nine-year-old rainbow princess who'd given me so much grief. Sometimes, as she peered at a hard line drive, I saw the serious, black-eyed, red-lipped gothy girl she was the day she left. So I played to them, too.

After a bunch of pitches, Glory turned around, smiling, wiping sweat from her face with the back of her arm. "Wow," she said.

And at that moment, I realized she *was* her mom. At the end of a song. Glowing. Gorgeous. And strangely magnetic. *Oh, man.* I had to leave. As sweet as she looked, I could not let myself get all tangled and jangled with a girl who might flip out at any moment. Not this summer, for sure.

"Glory!" Kayla called from beyond shortstop. "That's unbelievable. Your swings were so much better. And solid. Look how far you hit them!"

"I know. I could feel it." She turned to me. "I like that song, Andy! I like what it does to me. Can you keep playing?"

I began to panic. How, I wondered, can I get out of this? "Uh, well, actually . . ."

From behind me, out of the wild blue, I heard a voice I recognized right away.

"I like it, too! You both put on quite a show together."

Marlina Martinez, Glory's mom, had walked out of my mind—the last place I'd seen her—and onto the field. "Andrés," she said, "you must've grown a foot taller. How are you? How are your parents? I owe them a call."

"Fine, thanks. We're all fine." She had changed as much as Glory, if being thinner and looking lots prettier were the categories. Of course, I knew she'd been a teenage mother, so I wasn't too shocked at how young she looked. Still, it was hard to decide where to put my eyes. I settled on her knees.

She moved even closer. "I'm being totally honest about your music, Andrésito. You make that horn sing." We stood eye to mascara-rimmed eye. "Your grandfather must be getting really proud or really jealous by now."

"Oh," I said. "Thanks. But Grandpa passed away a couple years ago. His liver."

In one graceful swoop, Mrs. Martinez leaned over and pulled me against her bare shoulder and said, "Sweetheart, I am so sorry. I am *so* sorry to hear that. Gilberto was such a good man. He was so good to me."

"Yeah, thanks," I muttered with my cheek pressed against her coconut-oiled skin. "He was good to me, too."

She let go, stepping back to arm's length, and again I heard that old comforting sound as the shells clacked against the turquoise in her necklace. "We're still getting settled, but let your mom and dad know that I want to have you guys over. Okay? Real soon."

"Sure," I told her. But I told myself, I might have to be slightly busy that night. A little bit of Glory can go a long way. "They're playing at OB Juan's next Thursday. You'll probably see them then."

"Yes, I heard. I'm looking forward to it. Are you playing with them?"

I laughed at that. "No. I'm not ready. I mean, it's a bar and you have to be twenty-one and everything."

She dismissed that with a wave. "Oh, not true. I was working there when I wasn't a whole lot older than you and Glory. Technically, it's still a restaurant."

"Really?"

"I should know. I'm doing all of their accounting now."

"Whoa," I said softly. I squinted at her. "But Dad wouldn't let me, I'm sure. He really doesn't want me to—well, his opinion of the music industry is not that great. And he knows I'm shooting for the big time. I think he hopes I'll grow out of it."

Mrs. Martinez nodded and sighed. "Ah, the big time. It is ruthless out there. Even your grandfather would tell you that, angel. But it can be totally awesome, too. Of course, your father has his own ideas."

I decided to stop there, though I knew exactly what she meant. It's not like Dad ever said he was bitter or all that unhappy settling for being a small-time, small-town musician. But considering how far his own father had gone—playing with guys like Freddie Hubbard, Carlos Santana, and Tito Puente—I knew Dad would've liked to have done that well at least.

"I'll tell you what," said Mrs. Martinez. "I'll talk to OB Juan and see what he thinks, and maybe he'll mention something to your father."

"Really? You'd do that?"

"Absolutely."

"Well, it's not just me. I have a band, actually. We're a trio."

"That's cool. Doesn't matter. He'll either say okay or he won't. But I'll do my best."

She paused a moment and looked straight at me the way people do when they're thinking about something smooshy or nostalgic. I was bracing myself for an embarrassing comment or a wet kiss, but she just smiled, then turned toward Glory.

"Honey, I'm going to People's Food. Want anything?"

"We're low on soy milk," said Glory. "And I love those blue corn tortillas." Then she added, "But you can cancel the order I put in this morning, okay?"

"Which was that?"

Glory took a quick, but deliberate, look at me. "You know, the one about getting a cute guy to walk into my life."

Kayla squealed and slapped a hand to her face. "Glor-*ree!* Don't embarrass him like that."

They all laughed, though Kayla was the only one who seemed embarrassed. After all, she was normal. Meanwhile, I was already backing away. Don't worry, I wanted to tell Kayla. Five years too late for that. Instead, I said something about having to meet some guys for pizza and I left.

I decided that for the next couple days or so, I'd stay away from the park and the softball fields. Keep the low pro. I needed to isolate myself from Glory—and her mom, too. I mean, I couldn't believe how ready they were to invade my life. Besides, I had to stay focused on my summer mission—my musical career.

So, once I rolled out of bed around ten or eleven each morning, I'd grab my skateboard, sling my horn around my neck, and head west—away from OB Juan's—looking for music.

Some people play music by ear, but, me, I'd rather use my eyes. What I mean is, I'd skate along easy, cool, watching the street scene roll by. But I'd be scoping, scanning for rhythms, for a crow's hop, a dog's walk, slipping in eight, nine notes in a four-beat measure. I'd get in sync or syncopate, whatever it takes.

I'd be like a tagger, a spray-paint artist, like some muralist. I'd spray music out my horn, and it would cover people, cars, birds, buses, bikers, dogs, and trashcan cats—anything that caught my eye—as I skated on by, cool and easy.

Today around noon, I cruised down Bacon Street, aiming for Newport, the main drag through town, looking for something to play. Almost all of the old-school diners and coffee shops were on Newport, along with banks, bars, and tattoo parlors; thrift, surf, and antique shops; fast food, slow food, and Hodad's, where Mom worked, and the sign on the wall read "Under 99 Billion Sold," referring to the fattest, juiciest hamburgers I'd ever tasted.

"Bro!" called Freeman, who was sweeping the sidewalk in front of his hole-in-the-wall smoothie shop called Elysian Fields. "Rattle me something."

That's what I wanted! I gave Freeman a greeting blast. He wrote upbeat news for the *OB Rag*, so I caught his broomstrokes with a little "feel good" James Brown—*Bop* da-liddle-lit, *Bop* da-liddle-lit—as I rolled on by.

That woke the whole street up. My mom leaned out of the sidewalk window at Hodad's—balancing a tray of hamburgers and silver-metal malt shakers behind her—and yelled, "Andrés! Where's your helmet?"

I slowed down and hit my forehead with the heel of my hand, nearly knocking off my hat—a midnight-blue, thrift-store fedora—as if I'd completely forgotten to wear a helmet instead. Mom was cool—believe me, we had no major issues—except that she could be a real mother hen. Of course, we actually had a flock of baby chicks and chickens in the backyard at home, so maybe she caught it from them.

Anyway, I slowly brought my drive leg up, then in a flash I lowered it, pushing off and zooming past, while playing a few bars of a Mexican love song to her and all the people in the window seats munching on onion rings.

I jumped the curb and rolled across Abbott Street, where I spotted the Holy Jokester sitting cross-legged, yoga style, on the concrete seawall. He was an old Rasta surfer with black dreads, a big, blue star tattooed all around his left eye, and a permanent crimson smile curling up from the corners of his mouth.

"Drace!" he called, which was his name for me— short for Andrés. "I understand you're the magic man."

I skated up. "What? What do you mean?" HoJo always had some weird thing to say.

He peered out from under his dreadlocked bangs, which shaded his eyes. "I understand you have the magic touch with that softball player—Marlina's little girl."

I crashed my board into the wall, then hopped up next to him, sitting sideways. "How do you know about that? Do other people know?"

He pointed to his cheekbone, where the blue star began. "The night has a thousand eyes."

"But that happened during daytime."

"Okay, I'm busted, Mr. Trusted. The girl, Glory, she told me, mon. She said your music brain-warped her rhythm-ology. Made her hit like Venus Williams

smashing tennis balls crosscourt. What's the headline?"

"Glory said, 'brain-warp' and 'rhythm-ology'?"

"My words, Drace. Don't dance, mon."

"I'm not dancing. I'll answer, but first, man, give me
some time to be amazed. I didn't know I'd warped her."
I paused, conjuring Glory in my mind and wondered
if warping *her* brain would actually make her more
normal. "She wasn't looking for me or anything,
was she?"

"She was looking for the truth, Baby Ruth, like we
all are, eh? Give me your version."

"Okay, it was no big deal. You know how I play
stuff. She was moving and I was grooving—you know,
catching every little thing she did. I guess it made her
relax or something and hit the ball better."

"And you, Dracemon? What effect?"

"A strange one, now that you ask. I was definitely
tripping into the zone of the unknown."

He dipped his head and fell silent, then spoke to
the sandy sidewalk. "Sounds like the freedom zone."
He waved his hands like he was swatting bugs away
from his face. "That's all for now, mon. But I advise you
not to leave town, just in case we got anotta question
in your direction."

"Yeah, yeah, okay." I stood, laughing, and stepped
on my board. The Holy Jokester liked to use the royal
"we," as if he spoke for a great number of people. And

maybe he did—I wouldn't doubt it—but they were all invisible. "I don't plan on going anywhere." I pushed off.

"Wait!" he called. "You know the routine."

I stopped.

He lowered his voice. "We never had this conversation."

"Oh, yeah." I looked at him and raised my palms. "What conversation?"

He closed his right eye. "You're free to go."

He always said that. "You're free to go." Yeah, sure. Right after he tells me not to leave town. Dude was wack. But I did get some of my best song lines from him. For being a frazzled old guy, HoJo was still pretty quick with the wit.

Rolling south along the seawall, I watched a surfer shoot the pier, riding a nice south break through the thick pier pilings and out the other side. I painted every turn.

Under the stairway leading up to the pier, I spied a little old man with a black hat sitting on the seawall, leaning on his cane. I'd never noticed him around here before. In OB, people come and go all the time. Right on Newport there's a two-story international youth hostel that was always filled with foreigners. Probably where this guy came from. Wearing an old-fashioned black suit, white shirt, and a bright red-ribbon tie, he immediately made me think of Grandpa Ramos. Old country, old school.

That's a common thing I do—thinking about my grandfather. Or talking to him. Sometimes I'd skate along this wall and—I don't advertise this—but sometimes I'd talk to him as if he were sitting right there.

"*Mijo*," I would imagine him saying, "you need to build your passion, so your heart is pure and your purpose is one of honor. You must immerse yourself."

"I am, Grandpa," I'd answer. "Music is all I ever think about."

And he'd say something like, "Did I ever tell you about Wynton Marsalis? At your age?"

"A hundred times."

"Okay, amigo. But when will you hear me?"

"I do hear you. But my dreams are bigger than his were. I want to invent a whole new sound."

I mumbled the last part out loud, as I rode past the man in black, and he glanced my way. "Howzit?" I said.

He didn't answer, and I didn't expect him to.

I rolled into the beach parking lot, hearing Grandpa telling me to remember my roots.

Well, I thought, don't worry. I remember my roots, all right, but I also knew that Mom was still waiting tables at Hodad's, and Dad still ran his little music studio in a back alley behind this old retro-hippie head shop called The Black, and they only played out one or two nights a week.

"I've got plans to go a lot farther than that, Grandpa."

"Plans are talk, *mijo*. Dreams are talk. Action is what counts. *Acción.*"

"I know, *Abuelito*. This summer is my 'breakout summer.' You watch. I'm going to start my climb up the musical tree. And I'll swing on every branch until someday I reach the top." And I meant it.

Because, to me, it *was* so much more than talk. When I looked back through all that smoke in all those clubs, past all those blurry-eyed, old-school musicians, the losers, the cruisers, and the boozers who got chewed up, churned out, used up, and burned out, including my own mom and dad, I saw one thing.

I saw what it takes. And that's why I'd made my decision. I, Andrés Gilbert Ramos, was on a mission: to become a world-class trumpeter.

I skated through the asphalt lot, past the cop trailer, and headed for the alley. "How's that sound, *Abuelito*?" I asked him in my mind.

"*Muy bueno,*" I heard him say as I cruised toward my dad's studio, "but I only wish I could've taught you what you need to know, *mijo.*"

"You wish?" I answered, teasing him. "Wishes are plans. I need *acción.*" Of course, there was no answer to that. What was I thinking? The action was up to me.

At Dad's music studio, there was always work for me to do. I answered the phone, I booked bands, checked e-mail, helped bands set up when they arrived.

I cleaned up, recorded the sessions, even made the coffee. Anything to earn a few dollars and learn all I could about making music.

When I wasn't working, I'd still check in with Dad, to see if he had any vacant hours on the schedule. Whenever he did, I'd call up Tran and Lil Lobo, and we'd go in there and jam. Lately, we'd been working on my two best songs to burn onto a demo CD that I had special plans for.

"First two hours this afternoon are open," Dad told me when I arrived. "But don't just mess around. Use the time right."

"Yeah, we will," I said, punching up Tran's phone number. In a few minutes, both guys were there, and we got right to work.

After doing a sound check, I told them, "Soon as we finish this demo, I'm sending it to a big-shot radio guy named Dirk Sutro."

"Never heard of him," said Tran.

"Yeah, well, every night during the week, he does this show called 'The Lounge,' and a couple times each week he'll put on some national artist, some old-school jazz guy, maybe, or a new alt-rock group just breaking out, who'll come in and do interviews and play live music right there in the radio station." I paused a beat. "Someone new like us, *carnalitos*. I'm serious."

"Dream on," said Lil Lobo. He rolled his shoulders, which were made more massive by his sleeveless T-shirt. "It doesn't happen like that. We're new, all right. So new, we don't even have a name yet."

Tran leaned forward on the arm of the overstuffed sofa and strummed three heavy-metal chords. "Don't listen to him, brah," he shouted. Tran liked to use different voices and accents. "Send the man da kine CD! Do it now, brah! For you, for me."

"I'm talking," I said, nodding strongly. "Look, we go on the show, introduce our new sound to the whole world, become Dirk Sutro's next discovery, and we launch our career!"

Then my dad popped in and told us we'd better get cracking and stop wasting studio time. Everyone jumped. "Yeah, yeah," I said. "Just had to give these guys a pep talk."

But Lil Lobo paused for a reality check. "Papa Ramos," he started, "what do you think about your son's big idea, sending a CD to that radio show guy and everything?"

Dad only grinned. I knew his take on the hard-core music biz, and he was nice enough just to shrug, lift his eyebrows, and say, "Never know." But then he left the room. My dad was like that. I mean, after all, he grew up in the days of punk rock, when independent bands were the only true artists and to make a splash on the commercial side you had to sell your soul to the big labels and churn out la-la music. But he was cool about not spreading any of his negative views to the other guys.

I picked up my horn and played a bluesy riff into the air.

Da-dee-dee, da-dump! Doo-do, doo-do. Da-dee-dee, da-dump!

"You guys," I said, waving them close. Then I lowered my voice, so they'd have to pay better attention. "Don't laugh, but at our same age, Wynton Marsalis was already soloing with the New Orleans Philharmonic. I mean, sure, he was a little ahead of where we're at, but we'll get there." Then I pinged the bell of my horn with my fingernail. "You might say I'll be leading the charge. Into the *future*."

Tran "who-hooed" loud and long.

Lil Lobo only huffed. "Yeah," he said, rising up. "And I might say, you don't know *what* the heck you're leading us into, General Custer."

fusion charge
sk8rs rool

Later that afternoon, we scored another ninety minutes of studio time, and while the other band was clearing out, I was at the keyboard working on a chorus hook for a new song. I usually wrote my songs on a keyboard or a guitar, then added the trumpet parts later. Anyway, without warning, a great idea flew into my brain. It was so great, I sat back on the tall wooden stool to think it through all over again before I told anyone else.

"You guys," I said at last. "I have the perfect name for our band."

"Oh, you do, huh?" Lil Lobo had just crawled onto a pile of packing blankets we used for moving the equipment and was resting with his eyes closed. "What is it? Two Duds and a Stud? Won't that put all the attention on me?" He rolled over.

"No, no," I said. "Look, I'm serious. The Fusion Charge is led by us, right? So we rule. We own it and we rule it. And from that comes our name."

Lil Lobo opened his left eye and looked at Tran, who shrugged. Tran looked at my dad, who threw a hand behind his neck, exposing the flying eagle tattoo on his forearm. He laughed and said, "What name, *mijo*? We Rule?"

"No, no." Really enjoying this, I took a pencil and scribbled the words onto a songsheet. "See? Here. Fusion Charge Sk8rs Rool."

This time, all I got was silence. Then, in the middle of a yawn, Lil Lobo said, "Dude. I don't know. That's a huge mouthful."

"Yah, mon," Tran agreed. "I be trippin' my tongue on dat."

"Relax, this is just the formal version." I wrote some more and spun the paper their way. "But for short, we'll call ourselves this." I tapped the pencil above the words *FuChar Skool*.

I waited, but no one said anything. "Don't you get it? Dad, remember Grandpa was always telling me about the old school music? Right? So I'm giving him props, but I'm also saying, hey, we're moving on. That was the old school. This is the FuChar!"

"Oh, yeah," said Tran. "FuChar Skool." He snapped his long fingers, then placed his hand on the guitar. He played the rhythm of the name. "FuChar Skool. Fu*Char* Skool. Hey, the future's cool with *FuChar Skool*."

Pretty soon, they were all moving around, nodding, chanting the words and saying they got it now, they dug it. Lil Lobo started playing a steady horse-clop beat, kind of a *tick-tock, tick-tock*. "FuChar Skool," he whispered, then waited a measure. "FuChar Skool."

Tran fell in with a walking bass line, mid-range to low, kind of a *dune-dune-dune-dune, bah da-da,* that he played over and over again.

I hit the high range. A sharp blast followed by a trippy run, four quick notes, as fast as fingertips falling on a table, then Lil Lobo hit a double cymbal clap, and we were on our way.

And after a while, when we finally got back to practicing again, it was with a new fire. Dad even said he'd lay down a bass line for us on our demo tracks. But the FuChar Skool band would do everything else—drums, guitar, keyboard, trumpet, and vocals.

All was cool until we were almost ready to record the first track, and we heard a knock on the studio door. I grabbed the red SILENCE! RECORDING! sign.

"Sorry, forgot to put this up. It's probably Mom."

I pulled the door open. The vision we saw stunned us all and brought immediate panic to me. In walked the Martinez ladies, Glory and her mom.

They stood just inside the doorway wearing matching orange seashell necklaces, matching gypsy skirts, and completely unmatching makeup. Glory wore lavender eye shadow and purple lipstick, with glitter on her cheeks, while her mom wore dark mascara and eyeliner and reddish-brown rouge along her cheekbones.

"You need a set, gentlemen," said Mrs. Martinez,

stepping into the middle of the studio. "Look, I know you're working on a demo, and that's cool."

"You do?" I asked.

"Sure." She pointed with her thumb toward Dad, and I realized they must've already talked about us.

"But honey," she continued, "you need at least one forty-five minute, super-polished, ultra-tight, kick-down-the-doors type of set by next Wednesday. ¿Comprende?"

Tran had gone behind the glass partition to mess with the sound mixer. Through the studio mic he said, "What're you talking about?"

Lil Lobo pushed himself up from behind his drums. "Yeah who are you? And why Wednesday? And is either one of you seeing anybody on a steady basis?"

Mrs. Martinez ignored him. Glory grinned and wrinkled her nose.

"That's the Farmers Market gig," said Mrs. Martinez. "Newport Avenue, on Wednesday. I just signed you boys up. And a lot of people are going to be there. You know how that street gets on Market Day."

"You what?" I asked. My stomach was turning quite sour. "You signed us up to play for the street market?"

"You need experience."

"Mom hooked you up through OB Juan," said Glory.

Mrs. Martinez beamed a smile at Dad, who did not return it.

"That's no problem," said Tran. "We got two good songs already and a few more coming along."

Lil Lobo twirled his drumsticks before slapping them onto his snare—a cool move, actually—fully noticing Glory noticing him. "And you are?" he asked.

"I'm Glory Martinez." She tilted her head toward her mom. "This lady's daughter." Then she pointed at me. "And I grew up down the street from him, but we moved away, and now we're back."

Lil Lobo nodded with the tough guy nonchalance he practiced so much. "Okay, s'up? I'm Martín Rojas, but everybody calls me Lil Lobo."

Glory was digging this. "Oh, yeah? Why's that?"

Actually, I was curious to hear the answer myself.

"You ever hear of the big bad wolf?" he asked.

"Yeah."

"With the great big eyes and the great big lips and everything?"

"Yeah."

"Well . . ." He bobbed his head for effect. "I'm his son."

"Oh, *lobo*," she said, teasing him. "I thought you said, Lil *Loco*."

Tran jumped in. "Oh, that part goes without saying."

Glory kept it up. "Good. Because I'm a little loco

myself." She bent toward him. "So we should be good friends."

"We should."

All of a sudden—let's say it was a gut feeling—I did not like where this was going. I interrupted, saying, "Hey, flirt on your own time, Little Bad Wolf. This is studio time, eh, brah?"

"Oh, sorry," said Glory. "Mom and I just wanted to tell you guys the good news. We're leaving, right, Mom?"

Her mother smiled. "I'm ready when you are."

Glory started backing away, then put on the brakes. "Oh, Andy, before I go. I wanted to ask you if you could come by the softball field tomorrow. For a couple of minutes? You know." She whispered the next few words, as if hiding some embarrassing secret, "And play your song? My whole summer sort of depends on if I make—"

I stopped her right there, knowing where she was going and feeling certain she did not need me to help her make Kayla's team. Besides, my stomach had been in knots since she'd shown up, and now the knots were in knots.

"Glory, look, I'd like to, but with all this stuff your mom just laid on us—we have so much work to do. No way are we ready for a live gig. I was hoping to do a few open mic nights first, but we won't even have the time to do that."

"At least we have a name," said Lil Lobo. "It's, like, The Future Is Cool, or something. I forget."

"Shut up," I told him, then glanced back. "Glory, I wish I could help you, but I can't. Okay?"

She smiled softly, then turned away. Approaching the door, she said, "Yeah, sure. Sorry to bother you." She left.

By the looks I got, I could tell no one had any idea how much I hated saying no to her. Or the pain and complications that would've come from saying yes.

a total eclipse of the sun

The Ocean Beach pier is no social gathering place. Unless you like to fish. Or bop into the café for a stack of pancakes. Truth is, it's a good place to go if you want to hide out and hang out at the same time.

But we liked to go there at night—me, Tran, and Lil Lobo—after a huge day working on our music because there was always stuff we had to talk about, and it was a good way to unwind. Plus, if you went out far enough on that 2,000-foot pier, no one was going to bother you.

We'd sit side by side on the top of the concrete back of the last bench, way out on the west end. Several nights a week, right where the east-west lane runs straight into the T-wing that runs north and south, you could see three guys—three hoodies—in a row, with our feet on the seat and our forearms resting on our knees. From there, we'd just stare out at the blackness and talk.

Lil Lobo, who always sat between me and Tran, started off. "So, hey, Johnny Bravo, how long have you known those *chicas*, eh? And what did she mean—that Glory girl—about you playing her song?"

"Nothing. She thinks I have a song for her. Something that makes her play softball better. I tell you, I've known her since before I can remember, and believe me when I say, she's not all there—never has been."

"I don't know about that," said Lil Lobo. "She looked all there to me." He elbowed Tran. "You know what I'm saying, Tran the Man?"

Tran grinned, saying nothing, and lowered his head over his arms.

"And that was her mama?" Lil Lobo continued. "*Mamacita*. Looked like they were twin sisters."

"Yeah, but she's really cool, her mom. She will totally hook us up."

"Dude," said Lil Lobo. "You scored."

I just kept on rocking my head. I agreed. From way out here, anyway, it looked like a total score.

"So this Glory," asked Tran, "how lunar is she?"

"Oh, man. A total eclipse of the sun." I knew that question was coming. But there was no way I could really talk to these guys about how much Glory had troubled and embarrassed me when we were young.

"So, beware," I added. "Besides, we got a mission." Then I sang an old song. "All women is trouble. But some women is double. See 'em comin', you bes' step aside. A lotta men didn't and a lotta men died."

We all laughed at that, as if it were something any of us knew anything about. Felt better that way.

Soon we dropped back into silence.

After a while, Lil Lobo stirred an imaginary high-hat cymbal with imaginary brushes, using his mouth to sizzle out a nightclub sound. *Shheh, sheh-sheh-sheh, sheh-sheh-sheh.* Over and over again.

After he stopped, he hit me with a zinger. "You know something, man. I think your hopes might be set too high."

I was lost on a star just over the ocean, so I didn't clue in right away to what he'd said. But when I replayed the tape through my mind, I knew he was talking to me. He's challenging me on my dreams? I thought. Where was this coming from?

"People make it," I said. "You catch a break here, you catch a break there. My dad says OB Juan used to be really connected in the music industry. So, who knows? I mean, every day someone gets famous in the music biz. They have to come from someplace."

"I just mean, it's hard. So if you shoot too high . . . you know. It's a long shot."

"Oh, yeah?" asked Tran. "How long? From here to where?"

Lil Lobo played the game. "From here to that moon. That's how long. Or longer." He raised his arm. "From here to that one star out there."

He pointed toward the low, bright star I'd been studying.

"How far away do you think that is?" I asked.

"If it's still alive," added Tran.

"Couple billion light-years, easy."

"So, what's your point?" I asked. "We shouldn't even try?"

"No, man," said Lil Lobo. "We're going to try. You sent that CD off to that 'Lounge Lizard' guy, right?"

"Yeah."

"Okay. We're going to try."

That's all he said, and it felt a little strange to hear it. Lil Lobo was usually the cynical one, full of sarcastic one-liners, which was where I thought he was going with this. Then all of a sudden, his whole thinking changed. I decided the star had done it. Maybe he noticed what I once noticed: If you stare at a star for a long time, after a while, it looks like it's not that far off at all. Like it's really only an arm's reach away. But the thing is, you have to be foolish enough or naïve enough to risk looking stupid enough to reach out for it. In front of everybody on the planet. That's all.

After those guys left the pier, I hung out a little longer, skating slowly toward the shore, then stopping along the rail. For some reason, I liked looking at the backside of waves rolling in. It's not a perspective you get very often. But nothing around here is. OB's a town where millionaires walk alongside the homeless, but they look and dress about the same. In school, Mrs.

Ladd once told us, "Ocean Beach is the place where time goes to stop and think." I liked that perspective, since in most parts of California, time usually just races along.

From my house on Niagara, I totally get two points of view. I can look west and see 180 degrees of beautiful beach, rushing breakwater, blue-green sea, and a sky that goes on forever. If I turn east, I get 180 degrees of road sand and dust, apartment buildings, asphalt streets, cars, a telephone-pole jungle, and precisely fourteen bars, five liquor stores, and twelve softball fields—all within a mile of my house.

I skated on under the yellow-orange lamplight, thinking someday I should write a song about that. The yin and yang of paradise.

Rolling down the pier, I checked out the groups of fishermen huddled against the rails, speaking everything from Thai to Tagalog and from Spanish to Laotian. As I did, though, I barely noticed one dark figure stepping out from behind the little pump house and into my path. Before I could react, he had slid his cane between my trucks, locking my wheels and sending me dancing off my skateboard.

After four or five hard footstomps to catch my balance, I looked back over my shoulder at him. "Hey, dude! What's up with that?" I walked back to grab my board. "You're nuts, man."

It was the same old guy I'd noticed the day before under the pier, looking so out of place. Then he started talking faster than a rapper with his tongue on fire.

"Mr. Traveling Trumpeter Troubadour, please allow me to introduce myself. I am so pleased to make your acquaintance."

He reached into his inside coat pocket and pulled out a business card and waved it with a shaky hand just below my nose. "Max Lucero, at your service." He pinched the brim of his hat with gnarled fingers, tipping it at me. "I'm a great admirer of what you do. I've seen them all, from Satchmo to Miles—a hundred *gatos* with a hundred different styles. None like yours, though, my boy. None quite like yours. And I'm here to say I can place you into the greatest concert halls in the nation, into huge stadiums. On MTV! Under my sheltering wing, I can take you to the top of the charts and to the bottom of the hearts of every girl from twelve to one hundred and two. I am Maximo Lucero and I have been waiting for you."

Whoa. Under the glow of the lamp, I read the guy's card out loud. "Maximo Lucero, Promoter Extraordinaire."

That was it. No phone number. No fax. No e-mail. Just the dude's name, to which he responded, "At your service."

"Well, you practically broke my neck, Mr. Lucero."

"Call me Max. Please."

"Max, you almost killed me. Is that your idea of promotion?"

He slowly dipped his head, and I noticed his black suit had an elegance to it, rumpled as it was. Back in the day, it was probably Barcelona's best. And I could see myself wearing his thin, red-ribbon bolo tie. "A thousand pardons for my careless cane. My eyes are not what they used to be. I merely wished to gain your attention."

"Well, you got it."

"Marvelous. I can do much for you and your musical career, Andrés."

"You know my name?"

He flinched, pulling his head back, putting a finger to his chin. "Ah, well, yes. Who doesn't, in this town? But soon, the whole world shall know. The name, the man, the legend, the *sound*. This I will do for you."

I scanned both ends of the pier for any sign of Lil Lobo or Tran or the Holy Jokester. This was exactly the type of prank any of them would pull just to see me dance.

Once HoJo had pushed a wheelbarrow full of red-hot coals up and down Newport, asking the tourists for the fastest way to the sun.

"It's an emergency," he'd tell them.

Another time, on the seawall, I saw him hold up a jelly jar labeled "Charlotte." Inside was a spider. "She's lost, mon," he'd say. "She want go home." As the tourist backed away, HoJo would ask, "Hava you seen her website, mon? Charlotte's website? She worldwide."

But, if any of those guys were here, they were well hidden. From down the beach, I heard someone laugh—a long and crazy laugh—and right then I knew I'd been had.

"Oh, great," I said, kicking my board out in front of me. "Look, Max. Ha-ha. Very funny. Yes, I need promotion. Maybe you could help me next year in school. You know—get me promoted from tenth grade to eleventh? How about that?"

"But, of course." He politely stepped back and gave me a small bow. "Perhaps we can continue our discussion at a future date."

"Yeah, cool," I said, turning my board.

As I shoved off, he added, "Perhaps at a future school."

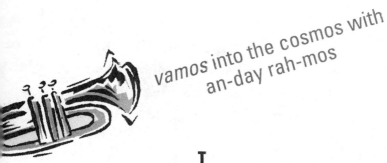

vamos into the cosmos with an-day rah-mos

The night, as the Holy Jokester liked to say, has a thousand eyes, and last night, as I rattled my way off the pier, I was sure most of them were on me. And one had a blue star tattooed around it.

But my run-in with "Max Exposure" did remind me that I had a bit of promo work to do myself.

Before I headed down to Dad's studio, I decided to call the radio station to check on the CD package I'd sent out. Promotion required follow-up. I knew that much at least. My biggest fear, though, was not that I'd leave a dumb voicemail or anything. It was that my voice sounded so young. Who would ever take me seriously?

Once I'd heard Grandpa tell an old jazzman that in his early twenties, he had such a low singing voice and sounded so much older because he'd already smoked cigarettes for about ten years and drank scratch-dog tequila.

Well, I had no time for that, not to mention no desire, after what alcohol had done to Grandpa's liver. But I did have some apple cider vinegar in the kitchen cabinet. And some red-hot Tabasco sauce on the table. I also found a couple of juicy lemons in the fruit bowl, a can of Coke and a bottle of horseradish in the fridge, and a jar of freeze-dried, instant coffee pellets on the counter.

"This just might work," I told myself.

So right before I made the biggest phone call of my life, I mixed up a tall glass of the blackest, dead-cat stinkingest concoction I'd ever smelled.

"Yo," I said, swirling the brew, watching the Coke fizzle up. "I'm going to leave one killer voicemail." Closing my eyes and holding my nose, I tilted my head back and took a drink. The red-pepper burn scorched me from my molars to the bottom of my throat. After two more big slugs, I filled my mouth with the stuff and started to gargle. I swished it around for as long as I could stand it—at least a minute—then I swigged it down, too.

"Blechh!" I coughed and gagged and spit long strings of black saliva into the sink. I pulled up the front of my T-shirt, wiping my eyes and mouth.

"That's nasty," I rasped into the garbage disposal. Then I lifted my head and said it again, noticing that my voice crackled with a certain rough-edged texture. "Thazz naa-stay!"

Man, I thought. I sound like a real bluesman, sounded like old Leadbelly or Lightnin' Hopkins or Ricky Fanté.

"Na-cw," I said, walking back to my bedroom, "I'ma gonna make dat cawl." I punched in the number to the radio station. But instead of getting a chance to leave my well-rehearsed message as I'd planned, the receptionist actually put me through. To the man.

"This is Dirk."

Instantly, my gut filled with gas while I tried to remember my opening line. "Mr. Sutro?" I coughed—my voice now was a cracked-reed saxophone. I lowered my head to deepen the tone.

"Um, hi, I'm—uh, my name is An-day Rah-mos. Rhymes with *vamos*. And I say, *let's go* into the cosmos with, uh, Andy—uh, An-day . . ."

I just stopped. There was a black orchestra pit of dead silence on the line. I squeezed my eyes shut against the hot prickles climbing my face and started slapping the top of my head, trying to think. "Uh, en-ah-way, I was wonderin'—I sent you a CD?" Then I belched—big-time, before I could cover the phone. And, whoa, it was bad! I know, because half of it came out my nose. I coughed to try to cover the sound. "Um, called FuChar Skool?" I coughed again, from throat pain, and for a moment I lost my bluesman accent. "Did you get a chance to—uh—"

"Hey, man, I get a lot of CDs flying across my desk. You're what, the A&R guy or something? What label was that?"

My hand was so wet, the phone began to slip. "No,

I, um—I'm not with a label—I mean, *yet!* I was hoping that—" Now gas started guttering and sputtering toward my other end. Man, I thought. I must have the nervous system of a pigeon. Then, all of a sudden, *whapp!* Sounded like a door buzzer. My feeble brain crashed. The phone slipped against my cheekbone and beeped.

"Oh, sorry, that's—uh-hum, I got ah-nuther cawl." I could feel two lines of horseradish Coca-Cola running out of my nose. "Ah'll hafta get back to ya." I stabbed at the "end" button three times before hitting it, then tore off my shirt and covered my face.

Whoa, I thought. That was too bizarre. What happened to my brain? I was not a shy guy at all, but I had never been so nervous in my life, even around Glory. I fell back flat across the bed, tossed away my snotty shirt, then slid off the mattress onto the floor, not believing what I'd just done. *Go into the cosmos? With Rah-mos?* Dude, I told myself, if Mr. Dirk Sutro ever does find my CD, he'll *vamos* that puppy right out the window.

And that's when I realized: This big self-promotion plan was not going to be all cool and easy. In fact, so far it stinks.

warily we roll along

My stomach was raw. Don't ever add Tabasco to a horseradish Coke. Be like fusing Tex-Mex with heavy metal thunder. 'Tis a fusion blunder.

I figured I had to get to the studio pronto, so I could forget all about the nightmare I'd just been through. After two more pit stops, I opened up all the windows, and left.

Blasting around the corner where the sidewalk meets the alleyway leading to my dad's studio, I nearly steamrollered Max Lucero with my skateboard. Nearly decked the little dude from behind.

"Whoa!" I said, skidding my board sideways, then wrapping my arms around him and carrying him along, to keep us both from tumbling. "Sorry, dude. I didn't see you."

He didn't seem too ruffled or surprised. "Andrés," he said, setting his hat level again. "A piece of advice. You must watch where you are going."

"Look, I'm sorry."

He wobbled his hand. "Oh, it's quite all right. No harm done." He gyrated his shoulders inside his suit coat, probably adjusting his bones. "We all go flying around blind corners from time to time, thinking we know what we are getting ourselves into."

"Well, I just never expected—"

"Tut-tut, my boy. It is a dim and distant memory already. But in the future . . ." He looked at me with a serious glint. "Say, for example, if you ever wished to contact an influential radio host to discuss your music. What then? Would everything just roll along as expected?"

My heart jumped. I was sure my eyes were as big as they could get. How did he know about that?

"I can do wonders for you, young one. Won't cost a cent." He smiled at me, pointing to the sky with his cane. "I can move the stars around, if that's what it takes." He whipped his cane as if he were swirling a sword. "All you need do is give me the word." Then he turned and once again made his way down the alley.

I waited until he had passed my dad's studio before I stepped back onto my deck and rolled along.

Glory must've known about our band practice that day because she burst into the studio just a few minutes after we'd all arrived, saying, "Andy, will you come outside? Please?"

I was not, at that moment, in the greatest mood,

still bummed about my phone call and freaked over my "run-in" with Max. "What for?"

"I know you said you can't come to my workouts, so I was wondering if you could just come out into the alley for a couple of minutes?"

That's when I noticed she had her softball clothes on and was resting a glove against her hip. Behind her stood Kayla, wearing shin guards and looking seriously like a catcher.

"Come on," Glory insisted. "My pitching tryout is coming up, and I really think you can help. Kayla's going to catch."

Lil Lobo was already up, heading for the door. Tran was right behind.

"You guys," I said.

"Dude," Lil Lobo called back. "Come out here two minutes and play for her. I want to see this."

In the alleyway, Glory had the correct pitching distance marked off—forty-three feet—and Kayla was now crouching behind a white cardboard "plate." She lowered one knee to the concrete pavement—one knee guard, that is—smacked her glove, and held out a target for Glory, who turned to me.

"Okay, Andy, here I go. Get ready to play."

Truth is, I was not much of a baseball guy. I never played past Little League, and even then I didn't pay much attention. But I did understand music. I understood dance, rhythm, and improvisation. So, giving in to the pitchfork demon of peer pressure, I leaned there against the alley wall and said, "Okay. Go."

Glory held the ball in her right hand, adjusting the position of her fingers several times. "I'm trying out a new pitch," she announced. "I wish I could release it right, but it's hard." She squeezed her eyes shut and drew in a breath.

"What pitch is it?" asked Lil Lobo, as if he knew anything.

"Basically, it's a drop curve that you release with a real snap while putting extra pressure with your last two fingers on the outside of the ball."

All that, I wondered, in a pitch? You don't just stand there and fling it?

"Use your legs," said Lil Lobo. "Drive with your legs as you come over the top. It'll help."

"I know," said Glory. "I'm really trying to push off my drag leg, but I'm thinking too much about the release point."

She stood with her feet slightly staggered, hands together, staring at Kayla. And she started. First she leaned her shoulders back, leaving her hips forward, while holding the ball low, against her pitching leg. Then she took a slight step back, swung both arms above her head and stopped.

From that position, she bent forward, and, in one complex motion, brought both hands down to her right hip again changed direction, bouncing her right arm into a big upward circle, arcing over the top and behind her. Then, as her hand whipped past her thigh, she shot the ball toward home.

Whoa, that's dance all right. And it's also blues, pushing into rock. Classic twelve-bar blues has three lines per verse. You sing the first line twice, four bars per measure. Then you usually finish the verse with a clever, one-line kicker. Twelve bars in all. Glory's pitching was: one motion; she repeated the motion; then finished with a big kick and release. Hip to high point and down; hip to high point and step; then her arm continued on around, behind her back, to an underhanded zinger. That's blues. And when you speed up the blues, it's called rock and roll. That I understood.

Whether she had driven her legs or not, I couldn't tell, but the ball sailed off way left, maybe two feet from home plate.

"Oh," she said, "that's awful! I have to remember to step more to the right." She used her toe to scratch a mark in the thin layer of dirt. "Andy, listen. The secret is in my hips. When my stride is off, it's because I'm not rotating my hips enough. And I have to really push off with my back leg, because that gives me added strength for added spin."

"*Verdad* that," said Lil Lobo, squatting between Kayla and Glory, and nodding like some pitching coach. "Quite true, quite true."

I ignored Dr. Softball and began bouncing to the beat she'd used. "Let me see one more."

Glory set up again. "Okay, watch. Here goes."

Her rotation and her stride looked fine to me—how would I know? But she still wasn't happy. "Not enough drive on my drag foot."

"But it's better," said Kayla, returning the ball. "Do another one."

I began to play, watching for big things first, then the little details. Trouble was, they kept changing. The next pitch flew low and wide left again. I kept trying. *Dee da-da-da dee da-dee.* No, that wasn't it. *Da-dee da-dee.*

Everyone else just stood there in silence, watching us work. Five pitches, six pitches. Wild pitches.

Glory hung her head and fell forward, resting her palms on her knees. "Ughh! What am I doing wrong? I'm just so worried about not being ready for Saturday."

"What's on Saturday?" asked Lil Lobo. "A big game?"

"No, it's the day I try out for Kayla's super-cool travelball team, the RaveRiders. They're only adding three players and they really need a pitcher."

"There's nothing to worry about," said Kayla. "You're *so* good. You made varsity last year as a freshman, remember? Now, just take a deep breath and relax."

Wait a minute, I thought. Shouldn't my music be helping her with that? Maybe because I was still feeling weird about everything that'd happened that day, I just wasn't connecting with her. So I tried a different tack. I started working with the tiny rhythm she used when she tapped her hand into her glove after each pitch while waiting for Kayla to return the ball. It was much more unconscious.

Whu-huuu. I started. Then I added the glove pose as she waited to catch the toss. *Da-whomp.* I repeated it. *Whu-huuu. Da-whomp.*

Glory had already noticed. I saw her bounce slightly to the rhythm. She caught the ball, but kept nodding her head. Before long, she began to pitch.

And I saw how Glory, like a gifted dancer, had taken what I'd offered and adapted it to her art.

Whu-huuu. Da-whomp. Whu-huuu. Da-whomp. Dee da-da. Da-whomp.

Get set, arms up. Arms down, arms up. Whip around and fire.

In between pitches, I played melodic riffs in the key of G around the basic notes I'd started with. And slowly, in front of our eyes, Glory stopped struggling. Her wild leg and arm motions calmed down. She moved now as fluidly as a long, south break through the OB Pier.

Behind me, I heard Lil Lobo say to Tran, "I don't

know what's going on, man, but that trumpet talks to her." Right away, almost without effort, another soft trill entered the song.

The pitches created a sweet percussive sound of their own—the smack of leather—as each ball hit Kayla's mitt dead center. After a dozen more, Glory bent over again, hands on her knees, catching her breath. Then she fell to one knee and held her bare palm against her forehead.

I glanced at the other guys, wondering if they were seeing what I could see. "She's crying," said Tran.

Lil Lobo whispered. "She is, isn't she? I hate when they do that. You never know what the deal is or if you had anything to do with it."

I had nothing to add. Dude was dead right.

Glory lifted her head. Now we could all see. Yes, she was crying—but through a big, red-lipped grin. Ah, relief.

"Hey, nice going," I called. "That was fun."

But real, true confirmation of my music's effect on Glory came from Kayla, who rose up to meet her. "You were throwing two hundred percent better." Kayla shook her head, coming closer, using her palm to wipe Glory's cheek. "I can't believe this."

I couldn't either. No, not Glory's response—as amazing as it was—but my own. I mean, I said nothing to anyone, but *my music!* Where did that come from?

Once I'd caught her rhythm, I was playing so carefree, so natural—and way better than I ever had.

"Andy," said Glory, sniffling a little. "That's just what I thought would happen." She started walking toward me, smiling, snapping the ball over and over into her glove. "Please, please come by tomorrow morning. I won't ever bug you again, I promise. But, *please.* Tomorrow's my last day of practice before my tryout. And I have to be ready. I have to show them how good I pitch." She read the hesitation in my eyes. "Please."

"Tomorrow?" I said.

"He'll be there," said Lil Lobo. "I'll get his butt there. What time?"

"No, no, wait," I said. "Look, man, we have way too much—" I stopped as an idea hit me. "Wait a minute. Hey, Glory, what about this? We're all set up to record. What if I burned you a CD that you could load onto your iPod or something? Then you could practice with it for hours. You could even go to sleep with your pitching music playing in your ears."

Glory's eyebrows rose as quickly as her smile flashed open. "That's even better! Oh, thank you, thank you, Andy. I love it. You're so amazing." She grabbed me by the shoulders and danced me around.

But that's when I found out we'd had an audience— or should I say, "odd-ience"—the whole time. On top of the second-story railing, which ran around the

Dharma Center, sat the Holy Jokester, cross-legged in his Master Yogi pose.

I wondered what he thought of all this. Would HoJo, the blue-starred eye in the sky, consider all of this a joke? Or was it somehow holy?

"**D**race!" called out the Holy Jokester. "And Marlina's little girl! That was opera, that was ballet. You gotta smoke-signal that wiggle and let thy people know."

"Hey, HoJo," I said, lifting my chin his way. "Now you know, brudda."

"Yes, I know now, yes, I know now, yes, I know." He climbed over the railing backward, holding on to the wooden post, bent his knees and lowered his hands, grabbing the ledge he was standing on. Then, flowing like a waterfall, he dropped his legs over the edge, let go, twisting in midair, and landed on the lid of a green trash bin. He sat down and slid to the ground.

Taking long strides, like a slinky cat, with his head back, talking the whole time, the Holy Jokester approached. "You two-oh are the dynamic duo. You have proven the grand theory of the universe, mon. Music and the game of baze-bull—and all of its children, like soft-bull, kick-bull, and over-the-line-bull are intrinsically connected. Intimately, infinitely, and cinnamirtly."

63

"I was just going to say that," said Lil Lobo, nodding and searching around for eye contact, like an actor waiting for applause.

"Dude," said the Holy Jokester, acknowledging the agreement.

Kayla stood stunned, eyes fixed on the old trickster, as he rocked his head, swishing his dreadlocks below his chin, causing the woven-in silver and gold charms and wooden beads to click together. My hunch was, she had never been this close to the OB icon before.

"How long will it take you," I asked HoJo, "to figure out what's going on between Glory and me?"

I got the blue-star, one-eyed glare. "More than a minute," he said. "Less than a lifetime."

"Good," said Lil Lobo, with a decisive, solemn nod. "That's almost exactly the amount of time we have."

Glory hip-bumped Lil Lobo to get him to shut up. Seriously, we all wanted to hear the Holy Jokester's take on what he'd seen.

"But I am willing and able," he said, "to lay my headline on the table. 'Crossroads Town in the Mix Again. Native Son and Daughter in a Cosmic Spin.' "

HoJo looked at Kayla in her pink Roxy top, her big, cracked-leather catcher's glove parked against her raggedy blue jean shorts, and the scuffed black shin guards covering her legs from the knees on down. "You have a cool, calm aura," he told her. "You are necessary to this environment."

Kayla took in a breath and said, "Thank you," while her eyes metronomed across HoJo with an uncertain beat.

The Holy Jokester scanned the rest of us. "You know the routine," he said.

Glory nodded. "We never had this conversation."

HoJo cast his hand into the air. "You're free to go," he said, and walked off.

As we watched him cat-slink away, Glory said, "I don't think he has any idea what's going on."

"Even if he did," said Tran, who suddenly came alive, "I bet he forgets all about it in ten minutes."

"Flippy dude," said Kayla. "But he is kind of lovable."

We all laughed. She was absolutely right.

"Okay, studio time," I announced. "Come on, you guys."

"Wait," said Glory. "Kayla and I are going to be at OB Juan's tonight listening to Olivia Olivetti's reading. Starts at nine. Why don't you guys come, too?"

"I'm in," said Lil Lobo. He darted his hand around like it was a flying spaceship. "I'm there. I'm waiting for you guys right now."

That cracked the girls up. "Andy," said Kayla, "what about you?"

Not likely, I wanted to say, though I'd heard about Olivia, the tarot card reader and fortune-teller, and her special once-a-month, full-moon readings on the cosmic state of OB. So I shrugged. "Well," I said, "if Tran goes."

Tran was so shy, I knew he'd give me a good excuse to lie low tonight.

"Tran?" asked Glory, turning to him. "Please? It'll be fun."

That's when I also remembered Tran was the politest guy I'd ever met. He grinned and laughed. "Well, okay. If you guys are going."

"We are," Lil Lobo assured him, wrapping his arm around Tran's neck. "We're free to go."

"Cool," said Glory. "We'll sit in the restaurant section near the front."

Still not believing we could, I said, "I thought we had to eat outside on the patio, with all the smokers."

"We can if we want. But it's not mandatory. We won't be at the bar."

Still hugging Tran, Lil Lobo said, "I'll buy the first plate of nachos."

"I like that," said Glory. "What time should we meet?"

I was already drifting my way back to the studio, thinking about the new track I had to lay down for Glory. "In more than a minute," I said. "But less than a lifetime."

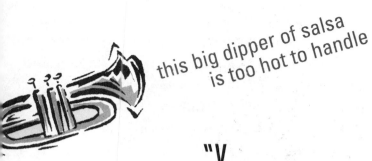

this big dipper of salsa is too hot to handle

"**Y**ou used to play some baseball, huh, man?" I asked Lil Lobo.

The three of us were on the pier again, leaning against a side rail about halfway out. The sun had set about an hour ago, and we were just killing time before heading to OB Juan's to meet Glory and Kayla at nine.

Lil Lobo smacked his lips toward the ocean below. "Yep. I used to be the hottest lefty in Peninsula Little League. They even compared me to OB's favorite son, David Wells, who played for the Yankees and everybody."

"Oh, yeah, right. You and Boomer are twins." Then I had a quick flashback. "Oh, man! You're Marty Rojas. Now I remember you."

"In the flesh." He stepped away from the rail and held his arms out wide.

"You were a year ahead of me in Little League and scared me to death." I turned to Tran. "Dude, about four years ago, this guy was famous. And not so ugly."

"*Marty?*" said Tran.

Lil Lobo grinned and held his arms out again.

"So that's why you think you know so much about girls' softball pitching?" asked Tran.

"I *know* I know so much. I was quick and clever and the heartbeat of the team. But as far as softball goes? The truth is—just among us three—I used to teach my little sister how to pitch windmill style, so maybe I watched a video or two."

"Well, the girls were impressed," said Tran. "You made big points today."

To that I added, with a dose of hope, "Especially with Glory."

"No, no, man," said Lil Lobo. "Not Glory. See all that drama? That's not for me. There's a term for her in baseball. THTH. Too hot to handle. I prefer to have my kissables predictable. She's the kind of girl you'd have to worry about all the time." Lil Lobo grinned and leaned my way. "Besides, I think she has a thing for you."

I pulled back and slapped the rail. "No way. Why do you say that?"

He falsettoed his voice. "Andy, please come and play mu-seek for me."

I couldn't help laughing. "Shut up. That's just Glory. How she's always been. You'd like her, dude. She'll pay a lot of attention to you. Besides, how can any girl be THTH for you?"

"*Carnalito.*" He buffed the back of my head with his

hand. "I'm Mr. Mellow. You should know that. Now, Kayla, she's—she's more my type."

"Oh, yeah?" This was news to me. "Well, don't say anything to her about it. You'll scare the poor girl to death."

He slapped both palms against his chest. "What, me? I'm harmless. You're so superficial, *carnal*. You only see my rough exterior."

Tran helped me out. "That's as much as we want to see, eh, brah?"

"Word to the third on that," I added.

Lil Lobo backhanded my arm. "Let's roll, man. Even if we're early. I'm starving."

"Now you're talking," said Tran.

Lil Lobo spun his deck around and pushed off. Tran and I followed at our own pace. As we passed the NO SKATEBOARDING sign, Lil Lobo suddenly peeled off, hard right, and slammed into the green rail.

"Hey, you guys," he said, pointing into the night sky. "The Big Dipper. Check it out. Looks just like a trumpet."

"Whoa," said Tran. "Yeah, you're right. Looks like a huge horn, man. Seems like three or four stars have been added or something."

Oh no, I thought, as I studied the constellation. Lil Lobo was right. That was not the Big Dipper I knew—not in its normal configuration. It was now a trumpet. It was as if someone had moved the stars around. Standing there, I felt as if a bony old hand had just squeezed the back of my neck.

"Strange," said Lil Lobo. "Never even noticed that before."

"Yeah," said Tran. "It's like there's three new stars on the handle to make the valves and two more rounding out the dipper to make the bell."

Lil Lobo resumed rolling. "I take that as a sign. It's a good sign, *'mano.*"

"Could be," said Tran, his head still tipped up in wonder. Then he took off. "But if that's a sign, it's the biggest billboard in the galaxy."

I kept looking, trying to spot the old, original stars among the newer ones, to see if maybe we were only being tricked into thinking it was a different configuration.

But just the opposite happened. As I watched, two stars began to blink, as if the trumpet's first and third valves were being played.

jousting with hockey pucks

At OB Juan's that night, Kayla was a far different girl than she'd ever been before. Wearing a short skirt, short shirt, and dressed to flirt, or at least cause some serious eyeball alerts, she could not stop fawning over Lil Lobo.

Tough break. For her and for me. I'd been sitting there thinking that if Glory and the wolf boy got something going, that would actually take a little heat off me.

"I like that blue top," Glory told her. "Looks cute. Where'd you get it?"

Kayla looked down at herself, and we all took another peek until her eyes came up again. "Oh, it's my sister's. She made me change clothes. I was walking out wearing this new striped green shirt my mom bought me, made from this crunchy material with UVA protection? And she's like, 'No way are you going out there with that on. You look like a cheerleader.' So I had to wear this."

Once again, three serious musicians took the opportunity to stare at her non-UVA-protected neckline hitting her tan line, then nod solemnly.

Kayla only shrugged.

"So," she asked Lil Lobo, "how do you know so much about softball?" Their knuckles rubbed while they both worked the cheese-and-beef-covered nachos plate. Well-centered on the red tablecloth, that dish had become the free-fire zone between two girls from Venus and three clowns from South Park.

Marty Rojas did not let her down. Sitting on my right at the end of the bench, he bobbed his head and neck a few times, aiming his black, wrap-around shades at her, and said, "I am a student of the game of base-ball, in all of its carnations." He ran a quick tongue between his open lips, then held the tip against his top lip, head-bobbing again, to express utter sincerity.

"Really?" she asked in awe, filling the word full of air, the way you might say it if someone had just told you he had a million dollars in a shoebox. "But pitching in softball is so different from pitching in baseball," she said, stating the oblivious.

Lil Lobo looked sideways at me, then, ducking his head, he peered on down toward Tran to make sure we were both paying attention, and I could tell he was not going to be mentioning his little sister's pitching les-sons. He might've coached softball at one time, but he was playing hardball tonight. Poor Kayla—or, as I de-cided her new name should be, *Qué Lástima.*

"Once you gain knowledge in one arena," said the little wolf, "it is so much easier to apply that knowledge in all arenas. I, for example, am also an expert on fashion. All over Point Loma High so many girls wear styles that are so last year, that I often suggest they remove the garment and—"

"You do not," said Glory, busting into a smile.

"I have in the past. I tell you, my knowledge in this arena—"

"Oh, arena, hyena!" This was too much for me, too. "Listen, hockey puck, nobody skates for free. If you know so much about everything in the baseball arena, then tell me the last time you saw a baseball moon."

"A baseball moon?"

"Yeah," said Glory, enjoying my challenge as well.

He bounced the bottom of the little Tabasco sauce bottle on the table. "Oh," he said, as if suddenly remembering a silly piece of knowledge. "Tonight. It's the full moon."

"Not even close," said Glory.

"Dude," I said, "that answer is *so* the day before the day before yesterday."

"Yeah?" he said. And right then Lil Lobo totally copped to his ignorance, which is one reason I'll always admire the guy. "I never heard of it, *'mano*. What is it?"

Onstage, someone tapped the microphone, and the speakers sparked. "Test," the guy said. "One, two. A little more bass, please." The band had set up and was ready to play, as OB Juan walked across the tiny dance floor and jumped onto the wooden platform.

"Tell you later," I said to Lil Lobo. "I want to hear this."

We all did, and Lil Lobo seemed happy to be off the hook.

OB Juan, a tall, wiry, dark-skinned man, with short-cut gray hair and a perpetual three-day beard, was dressed in a blue-sleeved baseball undershirt and faded jeans. He pulled the mic out of its stand and looked into the audience.

"Good evening, OBceans! Lend me your ears."

The bar side was pretty well packed and over the half-wall we could see the scruffy crowd whistle and roar at OB Juan's greeting, hoisting their beers aloft.

"These are great seats," said Lil Lobo, acknowledging Glory with a nod. "See everything."

Glory beamed.

"You know something?" OB Juan paced the stage as he started off. "My dear old papa wanted to be a fortune-teller once. True story. Bought a crystal ball and everything. But he finally had to give it up." OB Juan paused a beat. "Said he just couldn't see any future in it."

The moaning bay of the crowd nearly drowned out the *ba-dum-bump* rimshot from the drummer.

"You're killing us, Juan Quixote," someone yelled.

OB Juan shot back, "Surely, you joust."

Then another guy said, "Please, OB Juan, you are our only hope."

That brought cheers and a kindly wave from the good-natured bar-and-grill owner. "Okay, okay, I'm done for the night. But speaking of seeing any future, I predict the greatest fortune-teller in Ocean Beach will soon grace this stage, if you will all please join me in giving it up for Olivia Oli-*vetti!*"

As the ovation began, a tiny old woman with scraggly brown hair hanging out from the black-tasseled peasant scarf wrapped around her head appeared at the rear of the room. She made her way across the floor and to the side of the stage, where she climbed the two small steps one at a time.

Olivia Olivetti had been reading palms, tea leaves, and tarot cards in a little shop on Cable Street since before my parents were born. But only in the last year or so had she started giving her once-a-month psychic readings here at OB Juan's, on the cosmic state of the town. I'd heard they were really funny.

She grasped the microphone, and the entire room fell silent. Olivia held up a crooked finger and pointed to the rafters above the dance floor. Shaking and trembling, she screamed, "There is a mysterious force full of fire and death among us!"

The words echoed from the ceiling. She didn't move. Then, without another word, Olivia slowly hobbled offstage, still clutching the microphone.

"Whoa," I whispered. "I didn't expect that."

Tran leaned over. "I thought she was supposed to be funny. It's a comedy act, right?"

"I don't know," said Glory. "My mom says Olivia is really good at reading tarot cards. That she's for real."

At first, people were a bit uncertain how to react, but slowly I heard the chatter begin. By the time Olivia had entered the section of red booths where we sat, the band had gathered back onstage and were about to begin.

She headed straight for us, holding the mic up to her pursed lips.

"You two," she growled, pointing at me and Glory. Her voice boomed as people spun our way. She leaned over the table, squinting her gray-blue eyes as if focusing on a psychic vision between her and the plate of nachos. "I am also feeling a solemn connection between you two that grows in strength when there is trouble around, when the chips are down."

I peered directly at her, not wanting to look at anyone else. Oh, please, I thought, let there be no weird connection—solemn or otherwise—between me and Glory. Please be joking.

Slowly, Olivia reached in front of Kayla and Tran

and lifted up the plate of nachos. Aiming her mic at the table, she dropped the plate. The speakers *blammed* in our ears. "Now," she said. "The chips are down." Everybody laughed. Olivia did not rise; instead, she reached out and grabbed the very best tortilla chip left, the one I figured she'd had her eye on the whole time, with gobs of cheese and guacamole on it, held it to her lips, and chomped down, amplifying the crunch to the rafters and back. The crowd roared.

With a sly smile, she waved good-bye to all and handed the microphone to Tran. But right before turning away, she slapped down a single tarot card in front of me. The Fool.

By the time I glanced back up, she was trudging off.

I looked at Glory. She lifted her eyebrows and her shoulders, then let a crooked grin creep up.

"What's it mean?" I said. The card showed some joker in a colorful, triangular shirt and green tights, walking along on the edge of a cliff, whistling.

"Dude," said Lil Lobo, "she busted you, big-time. You da fool."

Tran ganged up. "Oh, sure. Like it takes a fortune-teller to tell us that."

"You guys," said Glory. "You don't know anything. The Fool is a very powerful card. He's someone who can do anything he wants because he doesn't have any fear. He's like the court jester who stands between two worlds, who's the only commoner who can make fun of the King."

"So it doesn't mean that I'm an idiot on the edge of disaster?" I asked.

"No, not at all. The Fool is really powerful. It's the crossroads card."

playing the fool and the american game, too

It wasn't that everyone understood the mysterious words of Olivia Olivetti, the Croatian fortune-teller who came to the shores of Ocean Beach during the 1960s, via Brooklyn, New York. Fact was, most OBceans were totally confused. But they liked the idea that the town was full of some shadowy force that was somehow linked to fire—one of the four basic elements and representing transformation—and death, which is the crossover part of life. That the mysterious force could be connected to me and Glory was something that only seemed to catch my attention. Everyone else thought Olivia's commentary was part of her act, though Glory did take the card seriously.

"I think you need to go see her," she said. "Olivia left this particular card with you for a reason."

"Yeah," said Kayla. "But don't knock when you get there. See if she knows when to open the door." That was a typical comment, and when I woke up the next morning, the whole deal didn't seem all that concerning anymore. Last night I'd also had a few random thoughts of Mad Max, the quirky lurker, but in the light of morning those seemed like a joke, too. In fact, I was thinking mostly about getting to the studio to work on our music. And once I arrived, I was all about the business of my mission.

I spent the next two hours listening to our latest tapes, fine-tuning and reengineering the sounds and effects. By mid-afternoon, I thought we finally had five, maybe six, songs in decent shape. I turned the speakers up and just sat in the engineer's chair listening to each one.

I didn't notice Mom come in, but when the tape ended and I shut off the machine, I suddenly heard a huge, "Wow." She was sitting on the arm of the sofa near the front door and shaking her head. "Andy."

"Hi, Mom," I said, using the studio mic. "You like it?"

"That was just you kids?" she said, walking toward me.

"Yeah."

She came around the corner and into the booth. "Those are remarkable songs for someone your age. Who did the writing? Who did the arrangements?"

"Me, mostly."

"All that stuff about freedom and fusion and those radical melodic bridges? That was you?"

"Yeah."

"Oh, wow. You really have something. I mean it. You're not only a good composer, but you're a poet, too. That will set you apart from so many other musicians."

Those words tingled. "Cool. But I think it's just because I listen a lot. You know, when I'm on the street and guys are talking, like HoJo and Freeman and everyone. And I watch and listen and catch their rhythms."

"Do you write those things down when they happen?" Mom sat on the stool next to me. She was dressed in her usual denim, with her dark blond hair pulled back into a jumbled bird's nest.

"No, but I take the ideas I get and put them to music in my head so I can memorize them and use 'em later."

"Well, you have a gift. That is not a very common sort of thing."

At this point I only nodded. Actually, I knew I had a gift, though I never talked about it. Over the years, in school and in the studio, I just started to notice that certain creative things came easier to me than to anyone else. My story lines always seemed more interesting. I could riff on a song after hearing it only once. To be honest, it s a little bit of a lonely feeling. There's really no one you can talk to about it—at least on an equal level. But it did give me the confidence to do what I was doing, and I hoped to take it as far as I could.

"You've got to play this tape for Dad, Andy. Or has he heard it?"

"He's heard parts of it, but not the final one."

"What'd he say?"

"Not much. The songs weren't really ready yet."

That was not the reason Dad hadn't gone all *American Idol* on me like Mom. It always seemed as if he didn't want to, or was afraid to, encourage me.

I think Mom understood. "Well, when you feel like it's ready, play it for him. But I want to be there when you do."

"Muy bien," I said, grinning. "But, Mom, why's Dad so down on success?"

"He's not. Is that what you think?"

"Well, whenever I mention my goals and stuff, he clams up or he's all, 'Success comes with a price, Andy.' And stuff like that."

"Well, the music business took a big toll on his own father," she said. "Cito thinks his dad lost ten or twenty years of his life by pushing himself too hard when he was younger, in order to make other people happy."

"You mean Grandpa was unhappy?"

She raised her finger to make a point. "Once an album was in the can and before the tour started—for those three or four weeks—Gilberto was truly happy. He was home, he was around family and friends. He loved that. And Cito loved that time the most. He really missed his dad when he went on the road. But work is work. And the bigger you are, the more people want from you. And the more they expect."

"So is Dad happy? I mean, are you guys happy with how things turned out?"

Mom's face softened and her eyes closed a moment. She looked totally serene. "Andy, we have it made. Honestly, I wouldn't trade this for anything."

I checked her for traces of a grin, but she seemed serious.

"Imagine, Andy, that we're looking out our back door. There's an organic garden. A little flock of chickens to keep bugs away and give us a few eggs. We have fruit trees surrounded by benches and chairs for when we barbecue and everyone brings their instruments over. I work about thirty hours a week, which is perfect. Cito works a little more, depending on business. The car's old, but it runs great and it's paid for. Back before you were born, and even after that, we always had lots of roommates, so we could afford to buy this house, and now it's worth a fortune. But the payments are pretty easy. We live two blocks from a beautiful beach in one of the coolest towns in America. What do you think?"

"Well, when you put it that way—sounds fairly excellent."

"It's not like we're geniuses or anything. We just followed our hunches and our hearts. And we decided not to play the American game. What I mean is, we're not consumers. We're not out to impress anyone with our careers. We'd rather live than work, instead of the other way around. So, yes, I'd say we're happy."

"Lil Lobo said maybe I got my hopes up too high."

"You know, that's what Grandpa Ramos told us when we decided to back off on the stress and strain of life in order to be happier. He thought it was impossible."

"Really? He said that?"

"He told Cito he was a quitter. He couldn't understand our thinking. But by the time Gilberto passed away, he saw things the way we did."

"Wow." This was a lot for me to absorb. "So what should I do? Mom, I really want to play music all over the world. I want to write songs, to play my new brand of music, to entertain people—you know, to be like Grandpa."

"And I think that's what your father's afraid of." She pulled me close. "Because it might put you out there beyond his ability to protect you. But don't worry. I know Cito. And he'll be behind you one hundred percent, no matter what."

"Even when I make it big?"

"In that case," she said, "he'll want to be there most of all."

After Mom left, I locked up, feeling drained but satisfied, and started skating down the alley.

The sun was whomping down on my neck and back with waves of heat. My eyes didn't rise above the alleyway as I rolled along and let the slap of my wheels hitting the cracks lull my brain into default mode. In other words, I was completely defenseless when I just happened to look up and see Glory skateboarding my way. In panic mode.

"Andy, something's wrong," she said, sliding to a stop. "I've played the CD all day, but the music's not working. It doesn't have any effect on my pitching and it doesn't even match what I'm doing. I really think I need another one."

I sagged. I knew I did—I could feel my chin hit my shoes. "Another CD?"

"No, another song. Today my rhythm's different. I'm more hyper."

That was obvious. She was bouncing her heels on and off the concrete. "Well, I can't give you a new song for every day."

"No, I know. Just for tomorrow. That's all. Tomorrow's the tryouts. And I know I'll still be all super-wired."

"You mean you want me to show up tomorrow and play for you at the field?"

"Could you? Please?" She looked so desperate. "It starts at ten. It'll be over in, like, an hour."

I took a deep breath, pondering whether I had any alternatives to getting myself far more involved than I wanted to be—and I came up with one.

"Okay, look, Glory. I have an idea." I pointed to the exterior studio wall, the bottom four feet of which were white cinder block. "Let me see today's style. I mean, what're the chances you have more than two pitching styles? So start practicing against the block wall, and I'll get the recorder set up so I can burn another song on your CD. This will be Style Two. Then tomorrow you'll have two to pick from."

"Yeah, okay." She looked as if she wanted to say more, but didn't.

I went back inside and dragged out all the equipment I needed. And though things did not go as quickly as I'd hoped, within thirty minutes or so we had something decent loaded into her iPod. And though both were similar, it did amaze me how different today's music was from yesterday's.

Glory gave it a listen.

"You happy?" I asked.

She grinned as she mimed a pitch and nodded beneath the headphones. "You're my angel," she said. "I know this'll work." She dropped her skateboard, grabbing it with her foot.

"And now," she said, "it's time to go visit Olivia Olivetti. Remember? And I decided I'm going to go with you."

"You did?"

"Yes. Otherwise, you wouldn't go."

Well, she was right. During the day, the more I'd thought about it, the more I felt like the whole thing had been a joke—just part of Olivia's act. "I was going to go later," I lied, hoping that would deflect Glory.

Her eyes seared me with the heat of a mind reader. "No, you weren't."

I made a quick calculation. Go now and get it over with or say no and give Glory one more thing to bug me about. Not a tough choice, Jack. Besides, I'd never been to a fortune-teller before.

"Yeah, okay," I said.

"Cool!" Suddenly, she leaned over close to me, brushed my cheek with a kiss, and in two pushes, was sailing down the alley.

In a weary stupor, I closed up shop again, while telling myself, Glory just kissed me, didn't she? Quick as a flicker of moonlight sneaking in and out of my room while I twisted the blinds, she had kissed me. Like she was totally comfortable doing that. Like she was my Aunt Hilda or something. Hey, maybe that's how she sees me. Maybe we go so far back, we really can't be much more than old friends to each other. And if she's going to act all relaxed around me, maybe now *I* can relax, too.

Considering the alternative, I would settle for that.

kat osterman sends me

We needed to stop by Glory's place before going to Olivia's, so she could change out of her softball clothes. All along the way, Glory would blurt out little plans she had for the future, as if I just needed to know this stuff.

"Someday, I want to play in Oklahoma City," she yelled, "in the championship game for the World's Cup of Softball."

I didn't even know they had one, but I was too far behind her to answer back.

As we rolled through OB Juan's parking lot, she told me, "Japan has a pro softball league that plays all year round. Pro teams in America only play during the summer. But they want to expand the league and the season."

We clanged to a stop at the foot of her stairway. "You want to turn pro?"

She scaled the stairs two at a time. "I would do anything. I would move to Japan. I'd move to L.A." She burst inside the apartment.

I followed and waited for her in the living room, reading the titles on all the CDs scattered over the coffee table and couch. Tell a lot about people by the CDs they own. I wondered who—Glory or her mom—had bought the Selena albums. She rocked. I totally loved Selena. She could mix her Tejano sound with . . . with anything and dance for you all *ha-cha-cha* at the same time. Grandpa said he never had a chance to meet her. Maybe he knew her now. That was a cool thought.

"Andy, come see my room!"

I tossed back the CD and pushed myself off the couch. Yeah, right, I thought. I really want to go see some girl's room. But I should've realized Glory's room would actually be something to see. It turned out to be a rose and lavender shrine. To softball. And, I noticed, to a Major League Baseball player named Khalil who played for the San Diego Padres. But mostly softball, starting with the bookcase of silver and gold trophies next to her closet.

Glory greeted me re-dressed in shorts and at least three clingy tops, judging by how many different-colored sets of straps I could count. But due to size, cut, and sheerness, she probably needed that many to cover what she wanted to cover.

"Sorry if it smells kind of softbally in here," she said, opening a window. "I need to do a wash. But I had to show you these." She stepped back and held up both hands toward all the posters on her walls. Olympic softball action shots ruled, sprinkled with a couple surfing photos, including one of Bethany Hamilton, and a huge shot of a shortstop identified as Khalil Greene—is "Khalil" even a name?—throwing out a guy at first base from a kneeling position. From way back in shallow left field. That pic was autographed.

I nodded toward a grainy action photo directly over the raggedy rainbow unicorn on Glory's pillow and the glittery wand stuck into her headboard. The shot was of a softball pitcher, mid-stride, with her arm whipping forward and her long legs driving—now that I knew what that meant. "Who's she?"

"Kat Osterman," said Glory. "She's on the U.S. National Team."

Fully aware of where I was, and being the gentleman I was pretending to be, I didn't say it, but this Kat was totally hot. Looked like some tiger-eyed runway model who'd jumped out of a glamour 'zine and landed in a softball circle.

Quietly, aiming for full-on sincerity and bleeding with the innocence of her little stuffed unicorn, I said, "She looks really good." I immediately decided to rephrase. "I mean, like a real good pitcher."

"I know what you meant," said Glory. She daggered a glare at me for a few ticks, then clicked into a smile. "And she is. My all-time fave. I saw her play when she was in college down in Texas and ever since I've had this dream that one day Kat and I would pitch together on the U.S. National Team, and one of us'll win the World Cup and the other would win the Olympic gold medal game." As she talked, Glory paced around her bed, windmilling her arm, throwing imaginary pitches, and sidestepping away from the walls, which were way too confining for what she had going on.

"Kat would be the team lefty, and I'd be the righty, and we'd just *dazzimate* the opposition with roll-off-a-cliff drop balls and seventy-mile-an-hour heat." She laughed at herself, shrugging her shoulders at me. "That's my dream, anyways."

I glanced at her ceiling and the other walls. "Are they all on the national team?"

"Yeah, mostly." She began to point. "Lisa Fernandez—she's a pitcher and, like, queen of them all. Natasha Watley is an incredible shortstop. She can cover a soccer field. Vicky Galindo. I love to watch her bat. She hits lefty and does this cool, running cross-step thing, but she's not a slap hitter. That's Jennie Finch and Jennie Ritter, two more great pitchers."

"Wow," I said.

Glory agreed, while eyeing them all again. "*Verdad* that."

And I now knew it was totally *verdad*. I had never imagined Glory's dreams to be so concrete, so true to life. But not until I'd stood in her room and saw the pitching charts and the ocean workout schedule—backstroke laps and running in thigh-deep water—taped to her closet door, her string of softball trophies, her photo gallery of stars, and her sweaty, but essential, clump of hats, bats, balls, shirts, shorts, shoes, socks, and gloves piled in the corner, could I ever have known. Glory had a dream and a passion as deep and as real as mine.

Olivia Olivetti did not direct us into a dark, spooky room with candles and incense burning when we arrived, or even to some crystal ball sitting on a pentagonal tabletop. She took us around to the back—the normal half—of her house, to the portion that had not been converted into "Madame Olivia's See Voyage." We sat at a glass-topped, wrought-iron patio table in a tiny kitchen straight out of the seventies or something. No microwave, no juicer, no blender. But she did have bright yellow cabinets and countertops, a pale green linoleum floor, fake fruit in the fruit bowl, and a coffeepot that sat right *on* the low gas flame at the back of her stove.

"I hoped you would come," she said. "Because I must tell you something very grave." She clasped her hands together into a fleshy white knot. "Those of us who have lived in OB for many years know. The great spirit of independence that pervades this town began long, long ago. It can be traced back at least as far as the tragic time period, centuries ago, when native peoples were forced to rise up against the foreign invaders."

I looked at Glory. Was she following any of this?

"When the king of Spain's soldiers came here with

the Spanish missionaries, they saw the native people living a good life. They lived free, in full harmony with the land and the sea. And, being practical people, rather naked."

I snuck another peek at Glory. Now, like me, she was following every word.

"But the strangers brought them just the opposite. They brought diseases and death. They brought impractical demands and complications tied to strange promises for their future salvation.

"On the afternoon of November 4, 1775, the Kumeyaay people from many villages gathered together, under the rising moon. Later that night, they attacked the soldiers and the missionaries. They burned down the church and killed three of the invaders." She held up three pale, puffy fingers and shook them at us. "A carpenter, a blacksmith, and a priest."

By now I knew what she was talking about. We'd studied some of this. The Spanish had come to California in 1769 to build a string of missions, straight up the state. But they were not your typical humble and polite bunch of illegal aliens. They occupied the land and brought a lot of misery—including beatings, torture, and death—to the local people. However, I did not know that the Indians had fought back and burned down the San Diego Mission, killing three people, including a priest. Teachers always seemed to leave out the cool stuff. But right away I thought, maybe that was why San Diego's baseball team was named the Padres. You know—as penance.

"All last night and the night before," she told us, floating her hand across the table, "I felt the presence of the same sort of invasion once again. And deception. In a dream, I saw both of you on the edge of fire. And you, my son, were being challenged to cross the abyss. So I say, you must beware."

"Beware of what?"

"Beware of those who wish to take away your goodness, who come bearing promises of future rewards. Nothing they can give you is worth the price they will ask you to pay."

She kissed the cross on her necklace and said, "This is all I know."

a beautiful, half-naked girl

"I don't know anybody who's offering me any rewards for the future," said Glory as we stepped back onto the sidewalk outside Olivia's. "Do you?"

"No, not really." For various reasons, I didn't want to bring up Max Lucero. Besides, he didn't exactly fit the description. Sure, he made promises of being able to help my career, but there was no price he was asking me to pay. Not a penny. And he sure wasn't asking me to cross some big abyss. "I don't think we have anything to worry about."

"Speak for yourself. I have tryouts tomorrow." She placed a sandal on her deck. "So I'm the one on the edge of a big fire."

"Oh, yeah, that's right," I said. We both started off. "Well, you'll do fine. Remember to take your music." I felt slightly guilty saying that, so I added, "And be sure to tell them Kat Osterman sent you."

"Maybe I will," she said, pulling ahead. "Thanks." She rode even faster down the sidewalk toward her house, driving with her legs.

Next day, almost noon, I was still in bed. My folks were already at OB Juan's having lunch and setting up for their gig tonight. They would be back home for dinner, then leave again. But me, I just stretched and yawned, pushing my feet against the sheets. I had a quick thought about Glory, and a nervous, CD-spinning whirl took over inside of me. Man, I just hope she makes that team so she and Kayla will be so busy practicing all the time, I can get back to concentrating on my music. I rose up and used my fist to smash a deeper head pocket into the pillow, then fell into it for another shot at sleep.

The doorbell rang. I looked at the clock and knew it was just Tran or Lil Lobo, stopping by for practice. I pulled the pillow over my head since they were about ten minutes early. Doorbells, I decided, need answering machines.

In a moment, the two-toned pipe-chime chimed again. "You guys," I moaned, pulling the pillow tighter. By the fourth time, I was fully awake and got up, stumbled over to my window above the front door, and yelled down. "Knock it off, brainsplatz! I already know you're there. You stink like scum breath all the way up here."

"Andy? Andy, it's me, Kayla." She backed up, out from under the porch canopy and onto the lawn. "I need to talk to you. Can you come down?"

I pulled back, away from the window.

"Oh, yeah, Kayla. Sorry." Then I had a nervous thought. "Are you alone?"

"Yes."

I stood there another second. I was in my underwear. I needed a shower. The place was a mess. "Uh, sure, I'll be right down. Couple minutes."

"Andy, bring your trumpet, okay?"

My trumpet? "Yeah, I will. I'm heading to practice, anyway."

I was still zipping and dressing as I dropped down the stairs. Pulling my shirt on over my wet hair, I opened the door and stepped onto the porch.

Kayla was in her softball gear. Her face, hot and sweaty. She grabbed my arm. "Come on!"

I ran with her. It just seemed like the right thing to do. "What s up?"

"Glory is, like, wigging out."

I felt my knees weaken.

"They had tryouts this morning. She was *so* nervous. Then, for no reason, these two other girls started making jokes and laughing at her. Like, 'Hey, *Gory* Martinez, when did you fly in from Venus?' and saying all this cruel stuff about how she pitched. It was so awful."

She jogged along, talking as if we were walking. I was panting like a dog. "Then at the end of tryouts, in front of everybody, my dumb coach announces the new players on the team and she doesn't pick Glory, and Glory just starts losing it. She starts slamming things and throwing softballs around. I mean, she freaks, until suddenly she gets all quiet and won't look at us or talk to us and then she starts climbing the backstop."

I stopped right there, pulling Kayla to a stop as well.

"Hey, Ramos!" someone—Lil Lobo—shouted from across the street. *"¿Adónde vas?"*

"No place," I called back. "Go to the studio, man. I'll be right there." I turned and lowered my head, now aiming my words at this brainy blond girl with the fiercest blue eyes. "Why'd you come and get me? I'm not the one to ask."

"Because you have this effect on her. I mean, I tried. We all did. No one else can get her to even move. Besides, she has a total crush on you."

I threw my hands up. "A crush?" *Oh, man.* This could not be true. What had I done to make Glory think I was crushable? She's my Aunt Hilda. "No, she doesn't," I said. "That's ridiculous."

Kayla regripped my arm and started off again, pulling me harder now. She was not messing around. "Come on, we're going."

Finally we reached Robb Field, and I was dying. I thought I had good, strong, trumpeter's lungs, but I was sucking air hard and fast. We stumbled down the bank, onto the grass, and Kayla finally let go.

"Oh, no," she said, staring into the distance. I

squinted toward the ball field and then I saw what Kayla saw.

On top of the chain-link cage of a backstop, twenty-some feet in the air, wearing only a yellow sports bra and lime-striped black Lycra biking shorts, stood Glory Martinez.

"I can't go over there." I said.

Kayla took a huge breath, stepped in front of me, and gripped my shoulders. "Andy, you have to. Please."

I actually saw myself in the blue of her eyes. I read a tenderness in them and—I am such a pushover—I knew I had lost.

I looked away, looked at Glory standing danger-ously close to the front edge of the backstop canopy. Kayla loosened her grip. I started walking.

People stood around watching, some with their dogs in tow, some leaning on bikes. I recognized sev-eral girls on the team, then spotted Tran and Lil Lobo, just rolling up. So much for band practice, I thought. Near them were three or four other guys from school, scoping out the situation.

As I walked closer, I knew they all saw me. And it was like I'd been transported right back to fifth grade.

Before long, there I was, standing in front of home plate, beneath a sad-eyed girl I'd once found hiding in the tomato beds of the OB Elementary School garden. I squeezed every valve on my trumpet, like a death grip. On the dirt near my feet, I saw her shoes and socks, her softball shorts and top, and her trembling shadow.

And then I really got scared. I didn't have to lift my eyes much to see another shady figure standing in the dark. Between the tall pair of bleachers behind the backstop, Max Lucero's eyes were fixed on Glory, as if he didn't even realize I was there.

In a slight panic, I made my way around to the rear of the backstop, turning my back to him. After tucking my horn into my waistband behind me, I climbed on. Can't believe I'm doing this, I thought, as age-old feelings of resentment zombied up inside of me. But what else could I do? "Glory, hold tight!" Hands to her sides, shoulders high, she stood rigidly, her bare feet gripping the wire links.

I started climbing, careful not to take my eyes off her. As long as she doesn't jump, I thought. If I can just get to her before she does something like that. At the top, I waited a moment to allow the huge structure to stop swaying. And as I did, Glory fell to her knee.

Slowly, I started to crawl. The whole backstop rocked with every move I made. Twenty feet seemed a lot higher from up here than it did from down there. "Glory?" I whispered.

Without looking at me, she said, "If you come any closer, I'm going to swan dive off this thing."

I had no idea what to say. The best I could do was, "If you jump, then I will, too. I swear."

"Shut up," she said. "Leave me alone."

"No, I won't," I answered. "I can't. Kat Osterman sent me."

For a moment, she froze, poised on that one knee. Then she collapsed to the canopy, on her side, pulling both knees to her chest. Slowly, I crawled along, inching along, until I could sit and then scoot my way next to her legs. She lay there, curled up like a seashell, and softly cried. I reached over to her bare shoulder.

She started choking out words into her hand. "I thought it would all be so different now. I thought everyone had grown up, and I could just come back here and start all over again new."

"I know," I said. "I know all about that trying to start again new stuff."

"But I'm *not* the same person I was, Andy. I'm not!" She sucked in air and sobbed it back out. "They thought I was a freak . . ." Her shoulders collapsed as she curled into herself even more. ". . . because I had to stop and listen to my music before each pitch." Then she laughed and cried at the same time. "I felt so stupid."

Oh, man. I had no, no, idea. How could I have put her into a spot like that? I should've been here this morning. What was I so afraid of? Then I realized that what I was looking at was exactly what I'd been afraid of. Glory getting so amped up—like I knew she could—then getting so wobbly, so unstable, that she crashes and burns at the slightest push.

"At least," she said, lifting her head slightly to look at me, "I still have you."

Me? My heart shrank in pain. How could she even think that? I had let her down so much. I was the biggest jerk in the universe. No, worse than that. I was a hollow tree.

Here she was, probably the most loyal friend I'd ever had, and I'd cut myself off from her—my very roots. I had made myself empty inside, exactly what Grandpa had warned me against. Right then, I could not have hated myself more.

I leaned back and fumbled behind me for my horn, for something to hold on to. "I'm sorry," I said. "I'm really sorry I wasn't here for you."

She shuddered in a breath and rose up onto one arm. Then she gazed off toward the bay, blinking, her ruby lips pressed tight, her mascara a streaky mess.

I wanted to touch her, to pull her close, but I didn't know if I should or how she would react. My eyes rode over her, and I noticed the tip of a tattoo peeking out of her sports bra, just above her heart. It was a tiny dark red rosebud, just about to bloom.

And in one of those flashes of brilliance that do not come from your brain, but only happen in miracles, I suddenly knew what to do.

An old, old song zipped into my head. I held up my horn and sputtered out a few bars. When I finished, a hush fell all around. I decided to play it again, but this time I sang a line before each bar, old school, like Satchmo, to blues it up.

"The Flower Queen is coming." I started low and rough. "Do not be afraid." I painted her with my voice, then echoed it with my horn. "The Flower Queen is coming. Atop a horse of jade." I added some Latin riffs, ending with a soft mariachi trill.

From both sides of the diamond, I heard whistling, cheering, applause. Lil Lobo yelled, "Yo, Andy! FuChar Skool rules!"

Glory laughed against a sob, and black tears shook loose from her lashes. "They like it, Andy. See? You're so good."

Her words filled me up. I played again, to the ball field, to the bay. I ripped it open and kept on going. Oh, man, I thought, Dirk Sutro should see me now.

From high atop that wild horse I played. *This*, I realized, is what I *want*.

As I transitioned from Latin blues into a mellower sound, she touched my arm. "Andy," she said. "Wait, wait a minute."

"What?"

She turned to see my eyes. "I'm sorry, too. I'm really, really not like this anymore. But when I heard those names, it was like—you know—like the old days. I just couldn't shake that feeling. And then I couldn't pitch. And then I didn't make the team." She cry-laughed again and held her palm to the sky. "So I climbed up here." She showed me a big wet smile. "You know, so I could rise above it all."

"Well, you did that."

"I know. It's what I always wished I could do." And she sat up, tucking her knees off to the other side.

I lifted the horn to my lips. "Want me to play a couple more before we climb down?"

She nodded, leaning against my heart side, and said, "Yes."

And I played. Her songs. All of them.

She was no freak. She was just super-sensitive. She was just Glory, rising to a level of honesty and beauty way above most people. And as I played, I began to see more and more, like a dense coastal fog had just broken open to reveal a lone bird crossing the sky, flying free and full of grace.

Because, man, you cannot believe how beautiful a girl looks when she's painted in music. How beautiful she becomes when she sings with you, when you stop and *open your eyes* to look at her, at who she really is.

Well, maybe she'd always been that beautiful, and I'd always been too blind to see. Anyway, I just kept on playing. One-handed. Old school. I had to.

My other arm was draped around this mad, beautiful, half-naked girl who had a crazy crush on me.

no woman,
no cry

I walked her home—well, to be accurate, I walked with Glory's arms wrapped around my elbow, while I carried my horn and her sports bag over my shoulder.

It turned out to be a nostalgic trek, as well. She brought up so many things I'd forgotten. "I remember," she began once, as we waited for two bike riders before we crossed Lotus Street, "when we used to sit—"

"—in the government yard in Trenchtown?" I interjected, quoting an old Bob Marley song.

She slapped my arm. "No, now hush. I was going to say, I remember when we'd sit on the pier railing, above the surfer lineup, and watch them catch waves. You always liked to see them riding the waves going away from us."

"Oh, yeah, I remember that. And you used to count one banana, two banana to see how many seconds the ride would last."

"Right! That's right. Then we'd walk down to the bait shop, and you'd buy a red Tootsie Roll Pop for me and a grape one for you."

Oh, man, I did remember—not just hanging out on

the pier, but that Glory and I used to have real fun together. "Yeah," I said. "That's right." It wasn't all as horrible as I recalled. I remembered that when we were just by ourselves, Glory could actually be pretty cool. Always saying something strange, but interesting. Or singing one of her silly songs.

"Hey," I asked, "where did the Flower Queen song come from, anyway?"

She hummed a note of easy remembrance. "Sometimes when my mom went to work she'd have to leave me with some pretty strange roommates who didn't always remember they were supposed to babysit. And if they left me alone or if I just got scared at night and couldn't sleep, I'd cover my eyes with my hands and after a while I'd see a lady dressed in pure white, wearing a crown full of roses, come riding out of the sky to keep me safe."

"That's a cool image," I said. "What did the horse look like?"

"All smooth and milky green, like it was made out of smoked glass. And it had a full, wavy mane and thick, muscular legs. Sort of like this jade pendant my mom had. And the lady would just sit on him, bareback, wearing this long, flowing gown with lots of ruffles, and never say a word. They'd just hover above my bed, making me feel safe enough to fall asleep."

After a few more steps, Glory reached up and touched her eyelashes with a fingertip, then slid the finger down her cheek, not realizing, or caring, that it left a black slash. She quickly sniffed and acted brave, gazing intently up Voltaire toward her apartment.

"I wish I would've known," I said. "You could've come to the nightclubs with us and slept with me."

Saying that made her smile and roll her eyes at the same time. But behind the joke, she knew what I'd meant. And now I knew something, too. For all that time, she was just a girl. I know she'd caused me misery and worry, but really, the whole time, she'd been just a little girl with a wild imagination and a single mom in a tough situation, and sometimes she got really scared. And at those times, she did the best she could.

"No woman, no cry," I said, which made her puff out a breath, since I was picking up the song again. "Little darlin', don't shed no tear."

"I won't," she said, shaking her head. "At least, not until you leave."

I took the beach route home. Didn't play my horn, though. Just rolled along Abbott, thinking about Glory.

The seawall was packed with the usual suspects. Bob Gnarly, intently reading a paperback folded in half, so no one could see the title on the cover "and report me to Homeland Security." It was usually a romance novel. Down a ways from him, Buzz Lite Beer was strumming away, playing a song by Sublime. A few clusters down from him sat the Holy Jokester.

"Drace!" he called. "Gimme the answer, Dancer."

He was pointing with both hands at his homemade tie-dyed T-shirt, which read, "What Would Scooby Do?"

"I don't know," I said. "Do about what? And what for?"

"None of that matters. Facts only obfuscate the truth. Mistakes are more important. They lead to progress and evolution. So don't dance, take a chance."

"Okay." I thought a moment. "I think Scooby would head down to Dog Beach and do a lot of sniffing around."

"Wrong!" said HoJo. Then, changing to a soothing tone, he added, "But you were very close. Please try again in a thousand years."

I cracked up. "Why do I have to wait so long?"

He looked at me, huffing, as if I were kidding. "I have billions and billions of people to ask before you get another turn, mon. Or did you forget about that?"

I shook my head. "Only for a minute."

"Ah, you must be in love."

Even from HoJo, those words were weird to hear. He gave me no chance to answer, though.

"She's pretty," he said. "She colorful. She's wild. She's brilliant. She's glory-ous! I say you two are a perfect fit. What do you say, mon?"

He was definitely way out ahead of me on this one. I thought a while before I answered. "Okay," I started.

"I say, we're still evolving. But if she comes by, brudda, you got to remember, we never had this conversation, eh?"

"I remember everything, Dracemon." His face broke out into a big smile. "You are the one who needs to forget."

"Forget what?" I said, acting as if we had never talked.

He tilted his head and wiggled his finger at me. "You are free to go."

"You should pay her," said Lil Lobo, "just to sit in the audience when we play. Serious."

"You think so?" I said. "I don't know, man. Why do you say that?"

"Tran," said Lil Lobo. "You tell him what you told me. What you saw."

"Well," Tran began, "what I saw the first time—the day she came by with Kayla—you totally outdid yourself. I never heard you thrill and trill like that, man. And I was thinking, right on. But today, up on that backstop with her on your hip, man, you blew everyone away. You were so good, you were scary."

"Dude," Lil Lobo added, "you were possessed. Like you were taken over by some mysterious force. You should've heard yourself."

"I did. I know. But why do you think that's only because of her? Ever think that maybe, after all these years of work, I might've had what is known as a breakthrough?"

"Oh, yeah?" said Lil Lobo. "Then why can't you be doing any breakthroughing during practice? Right here, right now. Today you're playing good, but you're always good. I say, bring her back. Sit her down. And let's see. But I think I'm right. Dude, I think she's your heart on fire."

"Yeah, yeah, talk, talk." And all stuff I didn't want or need to hear. I stepped over to the couch and pulled Tran's acoustic guitar from its case so I could ease out of the discussion by playing them a new song that was storming my brain.

"Look," I said, "we've got four days until the Farmers Market gig. Let's keep working on our songs. But, hey, if by Wednesday you guys still think I need to, I'll make sure she cruises on by."

My heart on fire? I thought. Glory? Actually, these guys could be right. But if so, I wondered, did I invite Glory's "mysterious force" inside of me—or did she invade?

Signs of Spring in the Air

OCEAN BEACH—Take a walk along Voltaire, up to OB Juan Quixote's, and you will see a banner shouting out, "I love Andy Ramos!"

Two questions may suddenly pop into your foggy mind. Who is Andy Ramos? And who loves Andy so much?

Okay, here's the deal. OB's Traveling Trumpeter has a new #1 fan. She is softball pitcher Glory Martinez.

OBceans have been treated to the street sounds of freestyle skateboarder Andy Ramos over the past year. But Glory and mom Marlina have just rejoined the OB community, and, like most of us, have been taken in by Andy's latest sound. Catch the trumpster next Wednesday at the Farmers Market, when Andy and his band, FuChar Skool, put a spell on you, and hear what Glory is shoutin' 'bout.

—**Freeman Jones, for the OB Rag**

had no idea what possessed her—had I ever?—but later that night, on the outside wall of their little apartment, Glory strung up a vinyl banner that read "I love Andy Ramos."

The tall red, blue, and purple striped words were visible to all traffic up and down Voltaire, which is a fairly busy street, running parallel to Newport. And though I got real good at looking slightly embarrassed in front of Glory and her mom whenever I stopped by, to be honest, I kind of liked seeing my name shining down from above. It was even cool seeing it in Freeman's *OB Rag,* the little once-in-a-while newspaper full of free coupons. I didn't mind the words, either.

At band practice I just laughed and strutted around all head-bop and stud-like when Lil Lobo and Tran started ragging me about it. They also managed to add the banner's line someplace in every song we played for the next two days. I'd be singing, "That's fun. Fundamental. That's fusion." And Lil Lobo would be all, "Just like pizza from Domino's, I love Andy Raminoes!" Then he'd slam the toms so hard he'd drop his sticks. Still felt good.

On Monday afternoon, Glory called and said she had to see me right away. So I met her near the beach at a cool outdoor taco shop called El Rodeo, located right below Ace Tattoo. Over a paper plate of chicken tacos, she told me, "Guess what? I'm on Kayla's travelball team. I'm an official RaveRider!"

"You are?"

"Yep. It was the weirdest thing, but her coach called me and said that another girl couldn't play, and that the team needed pitchers."

"But I thought—"

"Me, too. They must really, *really* need pitchers. But Kayla's the team's catcher and she told the coach, whose name is Becca—and she's so cool, despite everything that happened—that I was definitely a good pitcher and definitely a little too passionate about the game—hence the mountain climbing episode—but that she should give me a second chance."

"Wow. That's cool. What about those girls who were such jerks to you?"

"One of them, Dakota, came over and apologized to me—I think the coach made her, but anyway—" She shrugged. "And the other one didn't make the team."

"Wow, so it's all so sweet now."

Raising her drink, Glory took a long draw from her straw. "Yeah, well, we shall see. But Dakota's actually kind of nice. Her mom owns this workout center for women up on Muir called ShapeShifters. And Dakota said I could work out for free anytime."

Glory used my moment of silent reflection, as I ground down on a great taco, to bring up another, even bigger, topic. "Andy, remember when I asked you to come to my tryout?"

I nodded.

"And that I asked you because I realized I'm a much better pitcher when you're there—I mean, with your music?"

"Yeah, I know. It's weird."

"And I really hate even saying this," she continued. "Like I'm this emotional cripple and I have to depend on everyone else for support, but . . ." She took a breath. "I mean, I've really thought about this, and if it wasn't for softball—something I really, really love—then I would prefer the freakouts over having to depend on you or anyone else . . ." She stopped again. "Am I making sense?"

"Yeah, I think so. But keep going."

She scooted closer. "What I'm trying to say is, could you possibly help me out with your music for a little while longer? I mean, I promise, if I don't pick up or learn to do the stuff you help me with on my own by the Fourth of July, then that's just too bad. But I think I can."

I was still feeling so guilty over that day, I probably would've agreed to anything. But a couple more weeks didn't seem too bad. I took a sip of my *horchata* rice milk drink.

Glory began moving her hands with fingers spread wide, like she was juggling. "The whole deal in sports is that you repeat something so much that your body gets a sort of 'muscle memory' about it. And I really think I'll develop enough muscle memory by then to be able to establish my correct rhythm-ology—"

"Wait. Your rhythm-ology? Where did you get that word from?" I knew she'd picked it up while talking to HoJo, but I wanted to see if she'd admit it.

Her eyes opened wide as if she'd been caught copying someone else's homework. "I can't really tell you," she answered.

"All right," I said, narrowing my eyes. "You're free to proceed."

"Thanks. So anyway, if somehow you could actually come to all of my practices and games over the next three weeks—all the way through the Firecracker Tournament over the Fourth of July weekend—I would never, ever make you come rescue me again."

As much as I could feel her sincerity, I knew she was making a promise she could probably never keep. But I liked her thinking about muscle memory. It made sense. Do something over and over again, like tie your shoes or jump from octave to octave on the piano, or maybe even paint a girl pitching windmill style in order to launch yourself into a higher zone, and your body does, eventually, learn to do the task virtually automatically. "What's the Firecracker thing?"

"It's, like, the biggest tournament of the year. The Southern California Sixteen-and-Under Softball Tournament. And I need to do really well because that's the one that a lot of college coaches come out to see."

"Whoa. So that's big-time, huh?"

"It's a showcase event. That's what they call it." She began twisting the black and silver shells in her necklace. "So if you do really well, people start to talk about you as a top player, for scholarships and stuff. And I hate to think this far ahead, but if I pitch consistently the way I do when your music is warping my brain—" She covered her mouth, and this time her eyes said "Whoops." Then she shrugged and went on. "Anyway, if I do, that little secret scenario I told you about, making the national team and everything, could really happen."

"Then I'll do it," I said, and suddenly I began to feel a lot better. "That's no problem. Let me know your schedule, and I'll do everything I can to help."

Glory sprang to her feet, squealing. "You will? You really will?"

Everybody around us stopped eating, stopped walking—I think some people even stopped driving—to see what this tall, brown-skinned, totally ecstatic future Olympian in a bright orange midriff top was so excited about.

I felt honored just to rise up and let her arms entangle me. But man, she was talking about her dreams—a "secret scenario"—which sounded way too much like mine. And now that I knew what I knew about her, I had to say yes. And for the first time, we kissed. Gently, just touching lips. I was surprised how soft hers felt, how plush, how warm. Committing the moment to the top of my memory list, I decided it was okay that it ended too soon. Because this deal, this agreement between us, ran deeper than the whole crazy thing called love. This was based on friendship. You see, even by that time I knew you can hug and kiss and fall in love with anybody. But a good friend is hard to find.

groupies, loopies, and nutjob aliens

During the next week I got to where I really enjoyed playing at Glory's practice sessions. That was bonus time for me. In addition to working with Glory, I didn't realize how sweet it would be to have twelve cool and mostly hard-body girls welcoming me to the field every day, watching me, smiling at me.

It was like I had instant groupies.

And Glory had been right about her coach. Becca Hegel was a sweet former college softball player who was going to grad school for a master's in physical education. Okay, maybe she needed the education, but, believe me, she had the physical part totally mastered.

"I never got to thank you," she told me at the first practice, "for helping us out the other day. The music was awesome. And I feel so bad. I totally blew it." She was tanned, with surfer-girl legs and shoulders, wearing sunglasses and a white visor snugged around her straight brown hair.

"Oh, no," I said, lifting and pointing at my horn. "I was the one who blew it." She laughed, without realizing how much I truly meant what I'd said.

As we walked to where Glory was warming up, Becca said, "I don't know how the other teams will react, but you're welcome to come around whenever Glory pitches, as far as I'm concerned."

"Thanks," I said. "I'll try and keep a low pro during the games."

During the practices, though, I usually started out in high profile, on a bleacher board playing notes toward Glory and the field, as she worked on the sidelines throwing her sixty pitches a day to Kayla or one of the other girls. And I soon discovered that she had at least five different pitching rhythms—and possibly more to come. But I made sure that I always recorded any new beats and tunes onto her CD.

I didn't sit in the stands the whole time, though. Once Glory got into her groove, I'd break away for a few minutes and walk around the field, watching the other girls hitting or fielding or going through their practice drills.

And they always wanted me to play a song for them, to see if I could lift their skill levels, too. At some point during the week, I cooked up a song for each of them, but it never seemed to have any effect on anyone, except to start a giggle riot.

They thought it was a funny joke to spaz around and act all herky-jerky, challenging my abilities to paint them. Of course, they'd burst out laughing when I captured every stomp and pose, including the time when three of them lined up like marching robots, taking rigid steps, while crossing their eyes and sticking their tongues out in random order.

After a while, though, I'd always trot back to Glory to see how she was doing.

Once, Becca called me over to see if I could calm down Glory's stride leg, the one she lands on after delivering a pitch.

"Show me how you hold the ball," Becca was saying as I jogged up. She rose from a squatting position, then pulled her visor brim lower on her forehead.

"Like this," said Glory, who held the ball out in front of her. "Four-seam grip, but I do, like, a combo flip-drop and peel release."

"Yeah, that's okay," said Becca. "That works."

"Right. But I'm so focused on the release that my stride leg is all over the place. Side to side."

Becca turned to me. "She said you've worked on this problem before?"

I nodded. "Yeah, I did." Stepping back, I brought the tune up in my mind. "Show me a few, Glory."

Once I caught her essence with my horn, that was it. Her delivery turned almost effortless.

Becca, squatting again at Glory's side, looked back at me and said, "Your music definitely does something for her. I think it settles her mind in a way talking just doesn't."

I nodded. "I know. I mean, it must be something like that."

"Well, I wish I could put into words for all the players what that trumpet is saying to her."

"Yeah," I said. "I think music just has a bigger vocabulary."

On some days after her practice, Glory would come to the studio, and she almost always brought along Kayla and a few others, like Dakota, their shortstop, and Maggie, another pitcher. Did I play better? The whole *band* played better—way over our heads. It was definitely the greatest thing that had ever happened to any of us.

I also started to hang out with Glory at OB Juan's a lot. Nighttime, of course, was best, especially if none of our parents were there.

We'd sit in one of the old red booths, eating *nachos carnitos* and listening to the band while talking about the past, the future, and this weird thing that was going on between us. I told her all about sending out our demo CD to "The Lounge," and she told me about her dream of going to UC Berkeley and playing softball for the Golden Bears.

"Hey, you two," said Molly, the waitress who'd worked at OB Juan's the longest. "I saw Freeman's article about you guys in the *OB Rag*. You're starting to be the talk of the town. Can't wait to see your band play at the Farmers Market, Andy."

"Yeah, me either," said Glory.

Molly hurried off to deliver her order. Glory and I sat back in the booth seats, facing each other, staring at the half-eaten plate of nachos.

"What I don't understand is, what is it?" said Glory. "Why are we so connected in this strange way?"

"I've been thinking and thinking about that."

"Any ideas?"

"No, but I think that if we really want to understand it, we'll have to break it down. That's what I do when I hear a new tune, and it completely blows me away. I break it down, piece by piece, measure by measure, until I can see it perfectly in my mind."

Glory took a sip from her *horchata*. "Okay."

I searched the back part of my brain, near the top where I keep my memories of the past. "All right. The first time I played for you was while you were hitting."

"Yeah, at the park. And while you played, I got better at it."

"But no lasting effect, right?"

"Right. Same as when I pitch without the music. I go back to my normal skill level."

"But I don't play every pitch. So in between time, it still has an effect."

"Right." Glory's enthusiasm was beginning to kick in. "You just have to get me started, then correct me as I go along."

I weighed that. "So, you never start off with it. And

when you feel it, the benefit lasts for only a few minutes."

"No more than five. I've kept track."

I sat back, turning the information over in my mind.

"But what about you?" she asked. "What's going on inside of you?"

"I don't know. The music I play seems like it's really an extension of you, almost like you're guiding me to do what I do."

She brightened and leaned closer. "Yeah, that's what it feels like to me, too. Like it guides me. It guides what I'm doing. Like, all I have to do is follow the impulses."

"It makes impulses?"

She nodded. "Yeah, sure. I mean, it's music. All music has a pulse."

"Oh, yeah. But, wait a minute. When you walk or dance or whatever while I'm playing, and I start to mirror your movements with my music, my skill level goes off the charts. Isn't that pretty much the same thing that happens to you?"

"Yeah, yeah. But Andy, it's a loop. Think about it. The better one of us is, the better the other one gets, and on and on. But we can't do anything extraordinary without the other."

I slumped down against the booth back.

We fell silent. I'd thought we were getting somewhere, but we just ended up right back where we started. Like a loop.

"Okay," said Glory. "I've narrowed it down to one of two things."

"Oh, yeah? Number one?"

"It's magic." Seeing my quick frown, she waved her hand. "No, listen. Maybe there is no logical explanation. Maybe it has to do with forces beyond us."

"But it doesn't work on anybody else—remember? Wouldn't magic work on everybody?"

"I'm not sure. I don't know the rules."

I crossed my arms. "And number two is?"

"Aliens. We've been abducted by these all whacked-out, nutjob aliens who love softball, reggae, and Latin jazz and they're controlling our brains!"

"Yeah!" I said, nodding. This I dug. "Hispanic Jamaican aliens. Like some Rasta-cosmo Chicanos."

She shook her finger in glee. "From a parallel universe!"

"Of course!" I said. "From a place where the outfields are really out there."

We bobbed our heads together, our eyes locking, while we smiled like carnival clowns.

And at some point, in the middle of that glance, I caught a momentary glimmer in her eyes. We stared a bit longer, then quickly laughed again and looked away. It was the first time I'd ever seen that special glint, the one that can travel between you and someone else even across a crowded room. It may only last an instant, but it contains a secret message just between the two of you. Mostly it says, let's build on this moment later, when we have the chance, at a better time and place, but until then, we will carry this secret, this spark, just between us, tucked safely away, while we act like nothing just happened.

But at that moment I knew. Something had happened. In the middle of her laugh, her tease, her gleam—I had fallen madly in love with her.

PART II *the heartbeat of the town*

Listen, as the ocean pounds the drumbeat of the song. Listen, as the shutdown street, where the merchants meet, becomes the heartbeat of the town.

Peaches, oranges, nectarines. Llama rides, cakes and pies, and everything in between. At the Farmers Market, you never know whose path your path will cross. The best-laid plans entice and then get lost like ships astray. So listen to the ocean pound and the foghorn bay. You can sell your soul at these crossroads, *mijo*, or you can walk away.

wizardry built upon a mystery

Wednesday afternoon, before FuChar Skool's very first gig, Tran, Lil Lobo, and I met at the corner of Newport and Cable, each loaded down with musical equipment we'd brought from the studio or home. Down the block toward the beach, I could hear the band that was scheduled before us.

"They're still playing," said Tran.

"Good," I said. "Let's hurry."

And off we hustled through the marketplace, dodging face-painted kids munching on *pan dulce*, grandmothers with bags of fresh veggies filling their handcarts, and couples browsing black-velvet oil paintings of surfers and sunsets over the pier.

At the end of the block, we reached Bacon Street. That's the intersection where the bands set up, once the street is cleared at three—and tourist cars are towed without mercy. That way, all the vendors can take over with their trucks and tables. We pulled up just past a candle booth and stood on the sidewalk trying to catch our breath.

We were just in time. The music, which had been loud and bouncing, was now winding down for a fade-out finale. I knew the musicians, each from different bands, who all used Dad's studio for rehearsals. They really sounded pretty good. I began to feel amped, vamped, and totally ramped.

Lil Lobo pointed at Kayla and Glory across the street, returning from an ocean workout judging by their wet hair. "Look, there they are." He waved, and the girls immediately hurried over to our side.

"Wow," said Kayla, her eyes full of wonder, gazing at us. "I know some *real* musicians in a *real* band."

I had on an old blue work shirt, unbuttoned so that my tight red T-shirt would show off my tight abs, which didn't come from working out, but from being a skinny guy blowing the trumpet. Still, the shirt rendered me OB cool, with its territorial message, "There's No Life East of Nimitz."

"They look hot," Glory said to Kayla, behind her hand, but loud enough for all of us to hear. "What'd you guys say your band was called?"

"Future's Drool," said Lil Lobo. "It refers to our effect on women."

Immediately Kayla and Glory started coughing, stumbling around, claiming they didn't quite hear him right. "Future Fools?" asked Kayla, blinking wildly. "Future Stools?" said Glory. But it was all good. We needed the laugh.

"What songs are you gonna play?" Kayla had now regained her dreamy-eyed look.

"Who knows?" I tried to sound like some old spiritual improv master, so I held a finger aloft. "That's the thing with jazz. It's all wizardry built upon a mystery."

Kayla continued staring, but with her next comment, she won the honesty-in-commentary award. "I hate jazz," she said, lowering her eyes and glancing toward Glory.

"Me, too," Glory told her. "I mean, I used to. Now I like it. Maybe when you get older, you will, too."

Kayla punched Glory's shoulder. "I'm one year younger than you, Grandma."

Glory just grinned. "Fourteen and a half months, to be precise." She threw an arm around Kayla. "But I'll be sixteen in a few more weeks, and you'll still be a kid."

Kayla smacked her tongue at Glory and took in a sharp breath, then turned to us "real musicians" for solace. "Can you dance to it, at least? That's all I ask, is that it's danceable."

"Oh, baby," said Lil Lobo, "you two are gonna dance your booties off."

Kayla who-hooed and pumped her fists into the air. We turned toward the stage, all three of us grinning like goons, and got to work setting up.

But once Lil Lobo clicked off the tempo with his drumsticks and those two guys broke into "Translucence," our first song, I stood just a moment and took it all in. The crowd, the smell of fresh-cut oranges and mangos, the warm blue sky with a slight sea breeze, and us. Our *first gig.* I tried to imagine how we looked to all the people watching. A shy guitar player in sandals, cargos, and a faded T-shirt, who never looked up; a smiling drummer in sunglasses and a blue muscle shirt who rarely stopped scanning the crowd; and a skinny, thrift-store trumpeter, keeping beat with shaky knees and playing little musical blasts, while his eyes roamed the street.

But, hey, we were just warming up.

When the tune ended, the girls squealed loudly over the polite applause. Somebody whistled. But it was the jumping—Kayla snagging the vert prize—that drew our eyes and smiles their way.

"Thank you," I said into the mic. "We are FuChar Skool. Thank you." I stepped back, shared a cool flash-grin with Glory, then pointed the trumpet over the crowd. I blew a long, loud rhythm and blues note, on the one beat—a no-no in jazz, but we were fusion guys, right?—and Lil Lobo was on it. He followed with a strong, danceable, bluesy beat, then Tran's guitar joined in with a surprise—a salsa melody line that I let develop, then ran away with.

And Lil Lobo had been right. Kayla looked as if she could not stop her legs, dancing away. But she wasn't alone. When she stepped off the corner and danced her way into the street, a bunch of other people joined her. Including Glory.

I'd just had a strong beginning. I could *feel* the horn, as if I were somehow playing it with my whole being, my arms, my feet, my crazy legs. And here she was stepping into the street. Could Glory take my playing any higher than it already was? To be honest, it was hard for me to believe.

She didn't dance, didn't swing or swish her hips. She just strolled down the middle of the crosswalk in front of us with an elegant, athletic ease, her damp, curly hair falling like ribbons onto her strong shoulders. But I caught her.

I played her shoes, the skip and the scuff of her soles on the street grit. I played her hand at her mouth to cover a laugh. And it was at that point I lost myself. That is, I disappeared, and all that was left was this strange human conduit between the cosmic inspiration, or source, or whatever Glory really was to me, and the dazzling layers of sound that left my horn.

Suddenly, at the end of the set forty-five minutes later, I no longer doubted why I'd spent hours and hours a day, for years and years, learning and speaking to the world through this simple brass instrument. It was so I could be ready for a day like this. Ready for what Glory had just helped me achieve—no doubt.

As we took our final bows to an enthusiastic crowd—way bigger than I had realized—Glory yelled, "We love FuChar Skool!"

That brought a huge grin to my face, though I didn't

look up. And because I didn't, it seemed to prompt Kayla to yell even louder, "We are your total groupies! From now on. Who-hoo FuChar Skool!"

We all turned and stood up to laugh with the girls about that one.

I watched Glory walk closer, saw her easy, solid steps, her quick side-shuffle when a boy cut in front of her, saw her use her arms as balance bars, weight-shifters, as she nimbly regained her forward motion.

And for a moment it felt as if over the past hour, I'd seen so much of her, had read her so closely, that I needed to stop looking and allow myself to get back to normal.

As we packed up and moved to the far side of the intersection to make way for the next band, an older guy with bushy gray surfer hair, wearing a red flower shirt approached.

"Hey, you're the Traveling Trumpeter, right?" He was grinning like a truck-bed dog. "I must see you go up and down these streets ten times a day."

"Yeah, that's me," I answered. "I like to be outside where the action is."

The man closed in, right up to my face. Friendly guy. "What's your name?"

"Andy."

"Okay, I'm Moss Hartman. I book dance bands down at the Masons' Hall on Sunset Cliffs. You guys play some great songs. You have a card?"

"Uh, no" Why not, you dimmer switch? I slapped my shirt pockets anyway, pretending. "But we do have a CD." I turned and searched the empty spot where the equipment box once sat, then looked around for Lil Lobo. "Somewhere."

The guy didn't seem to hear or care. "Take my card." He lifted one from his shirt pocket. "Call me and leave your number, okay? I'll be in touch. Sounded groovy. We need bands." He left as fast as he appeared.

"Yeah, sure," I said to the guy's little gray ponytail hanging down the back of his aloha shirt.

"Well, hey." Glory was now standing beside me. "That sounded groovy."

I busted up. "Yeah, right."

"Well, it really did," she said. "Look, that's a start. He wants to hire you guys for dances."

"Yeah, that's what he said." I didn't have the heart to tell her what the guy's offer really amounted to. They needed bands, all right. That was code for "We pay you nothing, but, hey, you get exposure, and maybe sell a few CDs to the crowd, and everybody's happy."

I was well aware of how my parents' journey had started out—and I also knew the exact spot where their wheels had become stuck in the sand.

She put her arm around my shoulder. "Sorry I don't have a record deal to offer you, but I will help you lug your stuff back to the studio if you would join me later for an organic banana, mango, blueberry, and peanut butter smoothie at Elysian Fields."

"You kidding? Hand me my Traveling Trumpet case, please."

"Coming right up." Glory stepped away to retrieve it.

I flicked the man's business card with my finger, then tucked it into a pocket. He did say we played great dance songs. I may never see Moss Hartman again, but it felt good that he noticed.

mavericks don't run marathons

One thing I liked about Grandpa was that he used to tell me stories all the time. How it was on the road. Crossing paths with so many great musicians. Getting dressed for a concert in a sports arena locker room. Taking a hot, dusty bus ride one day, a limo ride the next. Road food, always stale, even on the day it was made. The thrill of a standing ovation. And the flowers—bouquets of flowers—his fans would throw onstage for him at the end of a set.

But there was one thing he never told me, though he had promised he would. "Someday," he said, "when the time is right, *mijo,* I will teach you what you need to know to make it in this profession. To make a name for yourself."

After dinner, I watched Dad swirl the dregs of his evening coffee, then set the cup down. The dinner plates were gone. Mom was in the next room talking on the phone and listening to Ray Charles singing gospel tunes. The only light in the kitchen now was an orange candle on the table. And sometime today I had decided that since Grandpa was no longer around, I would have to ask my dad the biggest question of my life, even though that question zeroed in on the only real divide there was between him and me.

"Dad?" I aimed for a casual tone. "How does a band ever break out? I mean, how do you get famous?"

He sat forward with his arms on the table. He interlaced his fingers slowly, leaving his thumbs free to touch and slide against each other. "Well, it's a long, tough road," he started. "I think what you might do is try to look at it like a marathon, where thousands of people start the race every day. And tomorrow there'll be a thousand more, just one day behind you. Of course, you can count on a bunch to drop out early, and you'll pass a bunch more along the way. But it's a race that goes on for years and years. And you have to hang in there."

Wow, I thought. He's really answering.

And he continued. "Your mother and I thought we could do it in five. Back then, that seemed realistic. But even before the five years were up, we knew—in our hearts we knew—we'd never get there. And when I looked at the bands that passed us by, the main thing I saw them doing was something I wouldn't do. Giving in and giving up."

"They gave up? How'd they ever make it big if they gave up?"

Dad wore a knowing smile. "Yeah, well, see, that's the part they don't ever tell you about. It's a different kind of giving up. Because, the thing is, Andy, to get anyone to put their money behind you, which is really what it's all about, you have to take your art in their direction. If you're okay with that and you're talented, they love you. They can package you. And they can sell you."

"This guy today," I said, "came by our gig and told me he needed bands for dances and stuff. Gave me his card. Moss Hartman."

"Oh, yeah, I know him. He's okay. Grandpa Ramos worked with him a long time ago in Hollywood on a movie soundtrack. But you know, he can't pay you anything."

"I know. But he said we played good dance music—and we really can when we have to—so I thought it might be cool if he hooked us up." I got an understanding nod from Dad. "That's what you're talking about, though, isn't it?"

"Well, it starts like that. Goes on from there."

"What should I do?"

"Honestly, Andy? I would play the dances, just to break in, get some stage time. You keep your eyes open with guys like that and you'll be all right. Just remember, the main thing is to go out there and have fun."

"I had fun today."

"Good. Keep doing that." He smiled, then lowered his eyes toward the candlelight.

"So is that it?" I asked. "Sounds kind of simple."

"Oh, there's a million ways to do it. Guys'll tell you war stories of what they went through, but it really just comes down to talent, perseverance, and a certain hunger—a feeling that you couldn't survive without working in this business. I mean, stories go from the Robert Johnson legend to these TV reality shows, with tryouts and everything. Who knows what'll work?"

"What's the Robert Johnson legend?"

Dad laughed and leaned back in his chair. "Well, he was an old bluesman from the Mississippi Delta. Down there they used to say that if you were hungry enough for success, you could walk out to an old country cross-roads at midnight and stand there playing the blues, and after a while, the devil himself would show up and tune your guitar. And from then on, you'd be a phenomenal hit. You'd have the easy money, women, and fame—all you ever wanted. Except for your soul. The devil would keep that for himself."

"Really? People believed that?"

"Well, according to the legend, when Robert Johnson was really struggling as a bluesman, he went off for a while, and when he came back, he was the greatest guitar player of his time. Even wrote a song about it called 'Crossroads Blues,' which was a big hit."

"All right." I piano-keyed my fingertips on the table. "Sounds like more fun than running a marathon."

Dad grabbed the back of my head and shook it. "A lot you would know about running a marathon."

"Well, you said having fun was the main thing." We laughed over that, while he admitted I was right. Then I sat back, and he sat back, and we focused on the candle flame in silence.

After thinking a bit, I said, "Dad? For you, is it still—I mean, do you and Mom still like to play out?"

"Yeah, I'd say so. And I think we always have. Having fun was never the problem. But the one thing I wish I'd never done was what I think the Robert Johnson story was really all about." He lowered his gaze, then peered back up. "You know what a maverick is?"

"Not sure."

"In the backcountry, there's a kind of wild horse that just runs free, goes wherever it wants. Never gets branded. And inside every good artist, there's one, too. A maverick. That's the spark that carries you along, that little bit of something new and unique that you want to add to the world of music. But I set mine aside in those early years, trying to get a foothold." He caught my eye. "You know, just trying to get steady work. I wouldn't give it up, though. I just figured that, temporarily, I'd set it aside. But, later on, when I needed it, the wild horse was gone."

"You had wild musical ideas?"

"I thought so."

"That's not fair. I mean, that you had to set them aside."

He shrugged.

"So you're saying that mavericks don't get much work."

"What I'm saying is, people in this business like a sure thing. They don't like free spirits, even though they might package you up as one. But eventually, if you're true to yourself, and you hang in there long enough riding your wild horse, you will get a kind of respect. Eventually. Most artists end up having to pick between the two roads, and they end up, you know, branding their maverick."

Dad pushed back from the table and stood. He took his mug to the sink and rinsed it. Before he left the kitchen, he stopped at the doorway. "But I'll say this, *mijo*. Every once in a while, a golden maverick comes along. That's a spirit, a sound, an idea that no one can stop. And a good musician, say, like a Jimi Hendrix or a Miles Davis, can ride that sound into the marketplace. And, like Grandpa Ramos used to say, if the winds are blowing just right, and the angels are lonely tonight, you might catch a break. And you might just break out."

Dad tilted his head, turning slightly, as if he were listening to what he had just said. Then he walked down the hall.

I sat there a moment staring at the orange crystalline candleholder and the amber flicker inside. A maverick, huh? Well, I think I definitely had that aspect in my music. But a golden horse? I didn't know. That seemed like a long shot.

I blew out the candle.

Mom walked in from the living room. "Andy, phone's for you."

I got up and made my way into the hall. "Dad," I called. "When can we use the studio tomorrow?"

"Not sure. Have him call you back in the morning."

I took the phone. "Hey, brudda."

Surprise of my life.

"Hey, man, finally got a chance to play your CD." Dirk Sutro's familiar baritone voice vibrated in my ear. "You're doing some innovative stuff. I like your ideas. And your drummer, he's got some chops. I hear a little Elvin Jones in there, right?"

"Yeah." My heart was pump-*pump*ing and my lungs were so frozen, I barely had enough breath to squeak out a single word's worth of sound.

"Well, hey," Mr. Sutro continued. "We had a last-minute cancellation for Friday night. So what do you think about coming on the show?"

"Okay."

"Yeah? You think you can make it? And bring your horn?"

"Yeah." My vocabulary was sincerely limited.

"All right, man. And the rest of your band? Think they'd be up for it?"

"Yeah."

"Good. All right. Look, we just finished our show for the night, so stay on the line, and my producer, Stacey, will come on and give you all the lowdown. All right?"

"All right."

"Yeah, okay. Nice talking to you. Hold on."

Where am I? I wondered. Standing in my own house, looking at a wall of family pictures I didn't even remember. I felt like I was dreaming that I was in a dream.

The producer came on the line. She was perky and nice, and so I relaxed enough to tell her what she needed to know.

When I hung up, I jumped, like, two feet into the air, shaking my fists.

"Mom, Dad, you guys!" I ran into the living room. "I'm going to be on the radio. Our whole band is. We're going to be on 'The Lounge' with Dirk Sutro!"

They already knew, I could tell by Mom's smile. She must've recognized his voice, too. Dad still had surprise in his eyes, but all he did was laugh a little and say, "Ride 'em, cowboy."

a hot and sticky situation

I had to tell Glory first. Floating down to my room, I punched in her number. "Glory, something so incredible just happened. You won't believe it when I tell you. But not on the phone, okay?"

"Okay, sure. What is it?"

"Not on the phone, I said."

"Oh, yeah, yeah." I could hear the edge of nervousness creep into her voice. "Why can't you just tell me?"

"I'm coming over, okay?"

"Okay, all right. No! Wait." I imagined her totally bent over fanning her face with her hand like she does, and pacing around her bed. "Our team's having a bonfire tonight. I'm almost ready to leave. Meet me there, okay? At one of the fire rings. I don't know which one, but just start at the lifeguard tower and go toward Dog Beach and look for us. Okay?"

"Cool, I'll be there." Then I paused and said, "Hey, I'm there already! I'm sitting there, bored to death, turning blue, waiting for you." All I heard after that was a screamy giggle and a click.

I really, really liked her.

I didn't have to find Glory or the fire ring. As soon as I left the grassy area and started across the sand, she and Kayla came running up.

"Andy! Andy! What is it? What is it?" Glory circled me, taking huge, dramatic steps in a big arc, pleading with her palms up. "I'm dying."

"She really is," said Kayla.

"I'm going to be on 'The Lounge.' "

"You're kidding!" She screamed and ran at me, leaping, landed on my feet, then tackled me onto the sand. The girl was slightly hyper. In a low, monster voice she said, "I cahn't bay-lieve it." She had both elbows against my chest pinning me down like she was champion wrestler Diamond Dallas Page.

"No, serious," I said, as normally as I could. "They want us—the whole band—to come out to their studio and play live. On the air."

Glory rose up and wiggled a finger at me. "I know what 'live' means, dah-ling. And that is so koo-well."

Seeing my chance, I sat up, too. "It's the start of my professional career. That's how I see it. We're going to be interviewed and stuff, we'll jam, they'll play cuts from our CD. I mean, *man*! So when he called—Dirk Sutro called me tonight, personally—and asked if I could be there, I told him, 'Yes. Absolutely.' "

"Well, *yah*," said Kayla. "And so you want to know if we'll be there? Absolutely, *too*. No problem!"

"I'm there already!" said Glory.

"Good!" I said. "It's going to be on Friday night. We'll have to get to the station by six-thirty."

"When?" said Glory. "Wait, which Friday? Next week, right?"

"No, in two days. I'm just filling in for somebody. Normally, he probably never would've asked me, but he needed someone at the last minute. For this Friday night."

Glory fell silent.

"Oh, no," said Kayla.

"What?"

"Our first game is Friday night. And Glory's pitching."

My jaw fell open, but before I could say anything Glory put her hand over my mouth.

"Andy, it's okay. I'll be fine. Really." She dropped her hand, but held me with her eyes for a moment longer.

"Oh, man," I said. "You guys, I was really counting on you being there with me. And, Glory, now I'm not going to be able to fire you up, either."

"Andy. Like I said. No big deal."

Maybe not for you, I thought. You'll have lots of games. But how often will I get a chance like this?

After a pause, I said, "I thought you guys weren't supposed to play until next week. You had a tournament or something."

"That's in two more weeks," said Glory. "Over the Fourth of July weekend. I gave you my schedule."

"Oh." I had never even looked. Tonight it hadn't even occurred to me. I mean, this was my career.

Glory stood and pulled me up. "Come on over to the fire. We have marshmallows. And chocolate bars. We need to s'mortify ourselves. That way, we can get over this stupid road bump without dying of malnutrition."

Sounded fine to me. Walking over, I was already cooking up a plan. "Tomorrow, we'll spend all day with each other practicing, okay? Both softball and trumpet, okay? And Friday, too. We'll do as much as we can to get ourselves ready."

"You know what we really have to do, Andy. Seriously. It's like I said. We have to learn how to do what we do without the other person being there. We just have to. I can't live all nervous like this."

"I know. Me either."

The rest of the girls on the team were sitting in beach chairs or lounging on blankets around the concrete ring, which was stacked full of old boards and a shipping pallet. A little pink boom box was snuggled in a beach towel spitting out gangsta rap.

"Nice fire. Where are the marshmallows?"

No sooner had I offered those words than my answer arrived. Dakota had taken a half-melted marshmallow and flung it at me through the fire. The brownish glob stuck to my T-shirt, right on my chest.

"Hey!" I pointed through the flames, acting all Joe Macho. "Don't be starting something you won't be able to finish, baby." That was not the smartest thing I could've said. Because about six girls with globs of their own had been waiting for a fresh target to show up. There might've been even more, but that's how many of the hot snot-shots got stuck to me.

"Oh, you are all going to pay!" I retreated, ducking behind a cooler, with Glory and Kayla. We quickly used my "arsenal" for return ammo. That started a war of the ring that went on for quite a while—until someone realized there were only a few edible missiles left.

"Truce! Truce!" called Glory. "I have to eat a s'more." Melted marshmallow was stuck to her cheek and neck and clumping her hair into dolphin fins Some girls looked even worse.

"I have marshmallow up my nose!" screamed Maggie. "And my eyelids are stuck together."

"Good," said Dakota. "Seriously, you look so much more attractive that way."

"Shut up! You die!" Fiery little red-haired Maggie spit-washed one eye open, and both girls ran screaming toward the water.

To me, it felt good to be exhausted. And to have laughed so hard. I rubbed sand on my stickiest parts, then cruised down to the ocean with Glory to rinse off. "I gotta go home," I told her, after submerging myself. "I'm freezing."

"What time tomorrow, then?" she asked, rather business-like.

"What time do you wake up?" I said, snatching her towel. I decided she was not going to out–early bird me.

She huffed. "I'll call you."

"I'll be there."

"I wish you could be," said Glory, ignoring the setup line. "I really wish you could."

rolling off into
the last unknown

The phone rang at seven o'clock in the morning, which was like the middle of the night for me.

"Andy. I had the worst sleep ever." Glory sounded hoarse, like she'd been crying. "And a horrible dream."

"Oh, no." I rolled over and brought the covers to my chin. "What was it?"

"I don't know. It was just little pieces. I was pitching. And they made me pitch from the top of the backstop. Like, the batter was standing on second base. And I kept telling them I'd only practiced pitching from up there once."

"Was I there?" Actually, I wasn't even here, being half asleep.

"No. But I kept, like, realizing I was missing something, like I couldn't find my glove, and more and more of my uniform kept disappearing, until I hardly had anything on."

My eyes shot open. "Are you sure I wasn't there? I think I was supposed to be there."

"No. Shut *up*. I was really crying. It was so sad. But people thought I was just putting on a show. Like it was a comedy game, so they were all laughing. And then I heard this horrible laugh, from this little old guy, dressed all weird."

"Dressed like what?"

"Just weird. I don't know. A black hat and a red tie and just weird."

"Oh." I sat up against my pillow, my heart pounding. Should I say anything? Even if it was all coincidence, maybe it was time to tell Glory—to tell someone—about Max Lucero. "You know, maybe that dream could have something to do with what Olivia talked to us about."

"Why do you say that?"

"It's just a—well . . . You know what? Why don't we meet someplace?"

"Can you come over?"

She took the dream right out of my mind. "Hey, I'm already there." I dug around my brain for another line. "I'm outside in a chair playing solitaire. I'm—"

She cut me off. "Andy. Not funny. Hurry up, okay?"

As I skated off to Glory's place, it hit me how much girls, even the good ones—like, in the humor department— were so totally different from guys in the emotion department.

I was painting a white dog with my music, while he sniffed his way toward the corner of Cable and

Newport, when who do you think I saw? Yeah, the dream crasher himself, peering into the front window of Starcrafts.

"Hey," I called, rolling up to him. "We gotta talk. As in, who are you and what do you want? And why do you know so much about my life?"

Max Lucero turned around and stepped forward, out onto the sidewalk, clutching his cane so tightly that his bony hand started making tiny circles in the air. "I've told you my business," he said. "I want nothing more than to help. And I know much about many people, merely by gazing at them." He started to shuffle on.

I ran around to cut him off. "Those answers aren't good enough. You knew my name, the name of my band, and all about the phone call I made to the radio guy. And now you're invading Glory's dreams. How do you know all this stuff?"

"It is my business to know things. You, son, need a backer who is in the know. I am the best there is. Simply the best. And with my gentle guidance, Andrés, one day you shall be able to say the same thing about yourself. And as for the girl . . ." His pale, cracked lips made a tight grin. "An artist always creates at his highest level when he is in love."

I froze, staring at this stranger with the craggy face, at his two moist brown eyes fluttering slightly above half-moon pouches of tired skin. Could I read any smcerity in those eyes? Any honesty? Or could I maybe detect a lonely angel who knew something about breaking out?

"You have a talent, Andrés, one which people notice." He gestured with his open hand. "So I noticed you. As many have, and more will do. And I can most certainly arrange for the right people to notice you at the right time. Not only Mr. Sutro or Mr. Hartman, but the power brokers of the industry."

He really did know stuff. "You can do that?"

"In an instant."

This all sounded so outrageous. But still, it was intriguing. I remembered the Robert Johnson story, wondering if it could be happening to me. "So, I have to sign a contract with you and everything?"

"Not at all. A handshake between gentlemen will suffice."

"And what do you want from me? I mean, what's in this for you?"

"Not a penny. You see, all I really want is your happiness and the distinct honor of presenting a unique, vital, and vibrant talent to the world."

I answered softly, in quiet wonder. "Well, that's what I want, too." But something still did not feel right. "I'll have to think it over and talk to my dad about this."

"What is there to talk about? Waiting will do no one any good."

"Well, first off, I have a big performance coming up

tomorrow night. And I don't want any distractions on my mind. Maybe after that we can talk."

"As you wish. But sometime tomorrow night, you may wish that your decision had been different. That is to say, how often does one cross paths with a man who offers to put everything in place, who can re-arrange events for you, who"—he touched the crook of his cane to his chest—"who can rearrange hearts for you, if that's what it takes?" He slowly winked. "By to-morrow, it may be too late."

He nodded once, grasped his hat and tipped it, then shuffled off

The freezing wave of cold that washed over me that moment carried a chill stronger than the one I'd felt last night, wearing wet clothes in an ocean breeze. I shuddered just watching him leave.

Was I supposed to think this guy could lead a golden maverick into the market? Or was he simply some do-gooder? Some promoter with a passion for in-troducing new talent? Well, I knew one thing. This dude's not normal. Even for OB.

"So, are you going to tell me," asked Glory, glancing into her refrigerator, "that my dream had something to do with the 'solemn connection' between me and you?'

"Might be, but I think it had more to do with an in-vader." Glory's mom had been up late and was still sleeping, so right then I felt like the invader. I talked softly. "Like that little old guy you told me about. What else do you remember?"

She wiggled her shoulders. "Wheww, I get goose bumps just thinking about him. Want some strawberry yogurt?"

"No, thanks. But anyway, did he say anything?"

"It wasn't what he said, so much." She shut the door, but just stood there. "It was like he didn't belong. Like he was lost—but not lost. Like he was from the outside."

"Outside of what?"

"Andy, I don't know." She closed the silverware drawer with her hip. "Like he was . . ."

"An invader?"

Glory plopped down on the couch next to me with a cup of yogurt in her hand, then set her bare feet on the small maple coffee table. "Sort of."

"And what about fire?"

She stared into midair. "I don't remember any fire. Why?"

"Just all that stuff Olivia said. About fire and this invader. I've—I've been having this feeling lately of being invaded." That brought a strange look from Glory, so I scrambled to explain. "You know, all these things about me and my goals are becoming so public."

She knuckle-tapped my head. "Hello? Mr. Wanna-Be-Famous? Are you in there?"

I pulled back, brushing away her hand. "I know, I know. Doesn't mean it feels good."

She scooped out another bite. "No, I know. But it comes with the territory. And there was no fire."

Then I realized what I was getting at. "Well, yeah, but I say being put on display in the middle of a big crowd is like being surrounded by fire, because you can't leave, you can't get out of there without being burned. Didn't you sort of feel like that in your dream?"

Glory bounced forward. "Oh, yuck, you're right. But it was like *I* was on fire. And everyone was watching." She reached around the couch pillow for something. "We should talk to Olivia. I'm calling her. We have to see what else she can tell us, okay?"

Like I had any choice. Glory's cell phone was in her palm and she was already clicking away.

After a few seconds, she glanced up at me. "It's her machine. What should I say?"

"You shouldn't have to say anything. I mean—"

Glory snapped the phone shut. "You're right. Besides, I can't wait. There's too much we don't know. Let's just go see her." She handed me her yogurt cup "Here, finish that."

Took me two bites. We grabbed our skateboards, then bounded downstairs and hit the street. But it was all right. I liked having Glory along, with her spirit of getting to the bottom of things. I liked not being so alone with—with a brain-invader named Max.

Olivia was real talkative that morning. "What is it?" she snarled, as her door squeaked open in perfect accord to her cranky voice. She had her eyes closed and was holding a sliced potato to her forehead. Finally, she peeked through one eye to see who we were.

"Children, please. So garbled are my messages. Bits and pieces, here and there. It is like hearing a cell phone that is all the time cutting in and out. And this migraine. I know simply, a man full of sadness has come for you."

"What does he want?" I asked.

"He has come for you. That is all I know. My head is pounding. I must rest." She eased the door shut, leaving Glory and me staring at each other in puzzlement.

"This keeps getting worse," said Glory.

"He's coming for you, plural?" I asked. "Or for you, as in me?"

"It could be me," said Glory. "What if he was the weird guy in my dream?"

"I seriously doubt it," I lied.

"Wheww." She shook again. "I don't like this. Let's go practice. Let's go do something. I need to work out. I need to swim. I need to stop feeling so scared."

Glory and I spent the rest of Thursday and much of Friday doing whatever we could think of to prepare for our "solo" performances Friday evening. Having half her team over to Dad's studio Friday afternoon turned out to be a cool way of doing just that.

It was just an informal jam to get everyone jazzed up for our respective events, although a few of the girls, led by Kayla, got a little friendlier with FuChar Skool, even me, than they had in the past.

But how could you blame them? The music was great. I was phenomenal. Sorry if it sounds egocentrific, but someone once told me, "It ain't bragging if it's true." And today, it was *muy verdad*.

So the girls got a little revved up? Like I said, who could blame them? I mean, other than Glory. She was mostly cool, but I did notice her eyes, a few times, moving into "fierce" mode and then, once or twice, into "pierce" mode.

At the end of the session, Madeline, the RaveRiders' left fielder, decided they should start calling their team the Ravers for short, and that after every game they win, we could throw a little rave party here at the studio. Not really going to happen, I knew, but I nodded support for the idea. I mean, she did have her arm around me—in a friendly rock-star-of-the-FuChar way. And they were all leaving.

Glory sort of floated up and wedged an arm in between us. Madeline vanished.

"Thanks for the party," said Glory. Then she added, "Break a leg." For good luck, right? Though someone else might've taken her dry tone another way. I felt totally busted, but decided I'd be better off playing ignorant.

"You, too," I said.

Then she pulled me in for a long, public hug. "Just don't break any hearts," she whispered.

At the radio station that evening, Dad helped us haul our gig bags and equipment cases into the elevator and then down a blue-gray carpeted hall to the studio. Luckily, we did not need to bring drums, but I did decide to roadie up Tran's acoustic guitar, in case I needed it. I mean, I was seriously ready to rock the joint and make my point.

Through the window in the door, I saw Dirk Sutro sitting at a circular table with chairs and microphones all around it. For some reason that sight sent my heart rate into double allegro. He talked into his headset while looking back through the glass wall behind him at the people in the booth.

Our escort, Stacey the producer, opened the door, and Mr. Sutro stood up. He was a lot taller than I expected and overall huge. He greeted us with a big grin. "Stace," he said, "we'll need a live mic at the table for Andy here and sound checks all the way around."

Again he looked at the techie guys through the glass wall, then concentrated on listening to something in his headphones that no one else could hear.

"Okay," he said to someone, then looked up and told me, "Over there in the corner we have a microphone set up for you and your trumpet. And you can see the guitar amp, snare, hi-hat, and kick. It's a little cramped, but I think you guys can make it work."

"Oh, sure." I unsnapped my trumpet case and was surprised to see how much my hands were shaking I could barely take my horn out of the case. What was going on? Nerves? No way. Here the studio was, filled with people hoping the best for me, and the airwaves were ready, finally, to be filled with my wild, maverick rip-oper-the-golden sounds, and I was quickly slipping into jitter mode on everybody.

My practice riffs were off-pitch and squeaky. I looked around at Lil Lobo and Tran, who both seemed incredibly everyday-like. Suddenly I wished Glory were here. I needed her impulse. How else would I get into my zone?

Tran walked up and bumped my shoulder. "What's the matter, brudda? Howzit?"

I kept wetting my lips, but I actually had no spit in my mouth at all. "It's okay. I'm all right."

I saw some bottled water on a small cart and took a quick sip. I blew another set of scales into the microphone. Sure, I was just warming up, but as the clock ticked by, I never got much better. Taking a few quick steps, I shook my hands hard, as if I were trying to shake off a bunch of ants.

"Okay, you guys," said Mr. Sutro. "One minute."

I sat down on the chair, leaned forward, and squeezed my palms between my knees, taking a few deep breaths. *Abuelito,* I said in my head. Where are you?

Mom and Dad were just outside the door, but I didn't dare look back and let them see how scared I was. The show's intro music—a cool Gilbert Castellanos tune—blasted into my ears, and again my heart jumped.

Mr. Sutro opened the show, building up our music and the songs on the FuChar Skool demo CD.

"Now, let's take a moment to meet the players in this experimental band, who are pioneering a whole new territory. I'll start off with the boy wonder himself, who's the source of this mesmerizing music we've been talking about, the young trumpeter, Andy Ramos, of Ocean Beach. Andy, welcome."

I gave him a quick nod, bumping my horn into the

mic, then realized this was radio, and I was supposed to talk. "Thanks."

"Great. Okay, then. So, Andy, you describe your music as a fusion, charged up with jazz, Latin, rock blues, pop, and almost any style you can think of. It's something you call the Fusion Charge or the FuChar for short. Can we get you to play us a sample of that rather eclectic mix? Maybe then you'll tell us how you first started experimenting with that sound."

I nodded and coughed, "Yeah, sure." I licked my lips, pulled my trumpet close, and closed my eyes. I then proceeded to create the weirdest sound my horn had ever made. Crackling, broken notes, with some real "creative" fingering, causing flats and sharps that I swear were supposed to be Glory's pitching song.

I had no idea what was happening to me. What could I do? I felt like I was under a spell to fail.

Finally, I just turned to Lil Lobo and Tran, motioning for them to jump in and play along. They did, and at last I could stop. But when I started again, my sound was still closer to a catfight than smooth, "mesmerizing" notes. The worst thing was when I saw Mr. Sutro drag a finger across his neck, asking Tran to cut it off, to end the song now. Within ten seconds, it was over.

"Andy Ramos," said Mr. Sutro, "and FuChar Skool are here in The Lounge tonight playing a sample of their wide-ranging fusion music." He looked up into the producer's booth. For what? A new guest? Maybe the guy who'd cancelled had shown up. Or the janitor.

"As I listen to your music in studio," he continued, "it amazes me how different you can make it sound."

Whoa. Understatement of the year.

He settled back down into his chair and began talking to me as if my grandfather were his guest. "First of all, Andy, it's interesting to me that you guys come from Ocean Beach with this no-holds-barred style of music. I'd say that when it comes to the national, support-the-corporate-culture-at-all-costs memo that got sent out in the mid-nineteen-eighties, OB was definitely not in the loop. They have a rep for being one of the most free-spirited, freedom-loving communities in America. A natural spot to give birth to your music." He looked at me. I nodded. "Wouldn't you agree?"

Then I said, "Yeah." I nodded some more.

"Anyway, when I listened to your CD, several sounds jumped out at me." As he talked, he signaled to the sound booth. "For example, track two, if you'll cue it up please, offers a blend of Tejano and, I don't know—Kid Rock?—that transitions pretty seamlessly into a trumpet solo. And that becomes sort of like a muted Miles Davis rendition of 'Oye Como Va', which, of course, is the Tito Puente tune that Santana made famous. Let's have a listen."

At last I could draw in a big breath, realizing that the radio host, the old pro, had just bailed out a super-nervous kid who had jumped into ice-cold water way over his head.

The rest of the show included interviews with Tran and Lil Lobo as well, discussing their approach to my music and the new songs coming along, and how both of them attack the improvisational parts of each tune. But there was no more live music.

My dad told me later that I added a few coherent sentences to the discussion, but all I remember doing is sitting there, with my trumpet resting against my shoe, and feeling on the edge of tears.

The show wrapped up with Mr. Sutro wishing FuChar Skool the best. After thanking everyone for coming in, he ended the hour saying, "And why don't we let the first track on FuChar Skool's demo CD, 'Fundamental Fusion,' take us out?"

That was a cool transition, as I heard the song rattle my headphones. But it seemed to me I'd already done that—I'd taken FuChar Skool all the way out of the music biz, and the music world, before we'd even had a chance to get in.

stage fright
of my life

All night long, every time I jolted myself awake, I had the same horrid thought. The angels had come looking for me, like Grandpa Ramos had promised, and I blew it. I wasn't ready for the break Dirk Sutro had handed to me.

My parents wanted to blame it on stage fright, saying it was no big deal, telling me, "Happens to everyone, Andy. It's all right. Go get 'em next time." Their tone, however, was less than convincing, and I knew they didn't quite believe it themselves.

Because it was a big deal, and I also knew it wasn't stage fright. I didn't get stage fright—at least, not once I started to play. Just hearing the first few bars is enough to send me to the improv room of my brain. And I'm happy up there, no worries, I'm tripping the lights. But tonight that room was dark and deserted, and I couldn't even find the door. It was as if someone else was interfering with—was brain-warping—my brain.

I could not stand thinking about the huge opportunity I'd just burned. Whenever I did, a sick, shaky feeling rose up inside, making me toss and turn and groan. Maybe, I thought, if I just got up and wrote a song about it—"The Radio Station Blues" or something—I could get rid of this urge to vomit.

I got out of bed and decided to get dressed. After weighing my options—like, should I roll out the window and off the roof?—I decided to climb out, with my guitar, and leave.

It was too late at night to work on a song in my room or on the roof, so I climbed onto the jacaranda tree, took a limb to the trunk, then swung down with one hand and dropped to the ground. I trooped to the end of Niagara, where the street turns into the pier, passed through the iron gates, and followed the pier out to the end, where it tees off into the north-south portion that I call the gull's wing. Did I really know what I was doing? Was I that desperate? Or that crazy?

Right there, I stood. Where east-west meets north-south. Where the pier makes a crossroad.

Wasn't much later, while I was putting down some song ideas on paper, using the top rail of the pier as my desk, that I suddenly realized how cold it was. June can really be a gloomy month. That's because the ocean temperature is still so much colder than the land that it creates a low coastal cloud bank people around here call the "marine layer." Tonight that layer was so low, we now had what people around here call "fog." From the end of the pier, I couldn't even see the café, the fog had settled in so thick.

All that moisture is no good for a guitar, but mine was already so old and well-traveled, I wasn't too concerned. Actually seemed to make the music sound bluesier. But I needed to work on the words, so I turned around and leaned the old ax against the bench behind me and turned back to my notebook.

Before I could re-focus on the song, though, I knew I had to clear the fog from my head.

"*Abuelito,*" I said softly, pausing with my pen over the rail. "I don't know what to do."

"What do you want to do, *mijo*?" It was as if he were standing right there, in the back of my mind. And that's where we spoke.

"I want to earn my spot. I don't want anything given to me."

"Who is giving you anything?"

"No one, yet. But there is a man. He knows things. And he makes big promises. What if they are true?"

"Do you trust him, *mijo*?"

"I don't know." I stared at the backs of the swells rolling toward shore. "At first I thought he was just part of a joke. But then he moved the stars around. Or he made us think he did. So maybe he's powerful. He said he only wants me to be happy. Maybe he's not a joke. And if he's not . . . What should I do?"

"What do you want to do, *mijo*?"

"I want to take this musical dream of mine—this strange range of musical fusion—and spread it all over the world. I want people to hear it, especially people who can learn from it and build on it and take it farther still."

"And being famous will do that for you?"

"It's the only way I know. The only thing I could think of to get my music out in front of the greatest number of people."

"How many people do you think will hear your music, build on it, and take it even farther?"

I thought a moment, noticing how the misty air had left droplets on the arms of my sweatshirt. "Just a handful probably. But that would be okay. Even just one."

"So, you think you will need this man's help to reach just one person?"

"Well, no, but . . ."

"*¿Pero qué, mijo?* What do you want?"

"I want—I want to be world famous. I want people to recognize me and my work. I want to make a difference. To be known as an innovator and really admired."

"Why didn't you say this to me the first time I asked?"

"I'm sorry." I hung my head as if he were watching me. "I was afraid. I didn't think you would approve. Sounds pretty egotistical. Like I'm only in it for myself."

"You think I would not approve because maybe I have told you before to seek a different approach?"

"*Sí, Abuelito. Sí, sí, sí, sí.* You did. But you never told me how. You said I needed to have a passion for music, and I think I do."

"But what else, *mijo*?"

"That my heart has to be pure. And my purpose, too. And to remember my roots. That from there my music will grow, and my career will, too, but I just had to know the way to do it."

"Do you have this pure heart?"

"Not always, I guess. I know I didn't have it tonight at the radio station. I was so full of myself going in there. Like I was already this great star."

"So, maybe the time was not right?"

"Nothing was right tonight." I stared down at the moisture now collecting on the pages of my spiral notebook. "But I *am* ready, Grandpa. I know I am. I think if I let this man help me, things will be better. He knows things."

"What things are these, my young one?"

"Good things. Big things. I can feel it."

"Why don't you go home, *mijo*? It's cold and wet out here. There is a fog. Tomorrow, perhaps, you will see things more clearly."

At that point, my mind just sort of shut down. I was done. I knew Grandpa so well, I could even argue his side of things—and then lose the argument. "I will Grandpa, I will. *Muchas gracias, mi abuelito.*"

I waited a moment, listening. I drew in a breath that became a yawn. The conversation had no more presence inside of me. All I really felt was a quiet sadness that "maybe the time was not right," no matter how much passion I had.

I never thought that when Glory told me not to break any hearts, she could have been talking about my own. I closed my lyrics book, wrapped my arms around myself and shivered, then turned to pick up my guitar.

Dude. I nearly dropped to the deck of the pier on buckled knees. If my heart had been broken before, it was sure kicking at full speed now. On the bench, right where my guitar had been propped, sat Max Lucero, holding my six-string on his knee.

a strangled man trying to scream

"Andrés," said the man in black. "I've been waiting for you. I hope you have had the time to think things over. And I do hope that you know by now I have been so enchanted by your music that I have already given you much support."

"What do you mean?" I walked toward him. "And I need my guitar back, please. I'm going home."

"Certainly." Max presented the old nicked instrument to me as if it were a jewel on a pillow, holding it faceup with both hands beneath it. "What I mean, Andrés, is, for example, I know that Marlina Martinez has recently become a big booster of yours. So isn't it marvelous, for your sake, that by good fortune she found a job and appropriate accommodations for her and her daughter right here in Ocean Beach, and did not have to settle in Los Angeles?"

I tucked the guitar under my arm and started hoofing it down the pier. "You didn't have anything to do with that," I said.

"I have something to do with many things."

"Prove it," I called over my shoulder.

"A difficult show for you tonight?" he asked.

That slowed me down.

"Perhaps it was not so easy to moisten your lips?"

I stopped and faced him, but the fog had swallowed him up. "What do you mean?" I called. "What are you saying?"

There was no answer. I already had a chill, but now I was shivering as if two bony hands had gripped my shoulders and were shaking away. I was about to turn again and start running when I heard him call.

"You can run, you can run, Andrés. But, please, tell this old friend why." His voice seemed to be moving, as if it were coming closer. Still I could not see him anywhere.

"Is it because you wish to go on doing what you are doing? Nothing wrong with that, I suppose. Start out playing small dance clubs, taking it easy, moving ahead slowly, but surely. That is, unless you should get stuck in the sand."

He appeared at the railing directly to my right. "I will tell you a story, if I may, about a man with lots of money, who produced many grand shows on Broadway and owned several businesses, including a baseball team."

I kept walking, but so did Max—and he was moving a lot smoother tonight than he ever had before. "One day some people asked him to back a new show.

A very promising musical. The man agreed and soon raised four hundred and twenty-five thousand dollars. And all he had to do was to sell one of his ballplayers. This man, Mr. Harry Frazee, owned the Boston Red Sox, and he decided to sell Babe Ruth to the New York Yankees."

"And you had something to do with that?" I stopped to face him.

He slowly closed his eyes, as if remembering a happy moment, then reopened them to say, "I shall go on to my point. Mr. Frazee gave his friends on Broadway what they needed. Not money, but *confidence*. Why let a radio microphone fluster you, for example? Harry Frazee provided his people with faith, with confidence. That's what I, as your backer, can do for you."

"I thought the Babe Ruth deal was cursed or something like that."

"*Au contraire,* my dear boy. The musical show was a whopping success. And Babe Ruth himself went on to become a whopping success. Everyone involved in the bargain made money. How can you argue with that? You wish to be successful, don't you?"

"Well, sure."

"You have a unique sound."

"I know I do. I mean, not to sound arrogant, but I realize my sound is interesting and unique."

"People need to hear it. For that you need me, a promoter extraordinaire."

"I know. I mean, people do need to hear it. And I'm horrible at promotion."

"Well, then. What are you waiting for? No one is asking you for money or to sell Babe Ruth."

"Right, I know."

"So, do we have an agreement?"

The chill was cutting deeper, into my spine. Olivia's warning about accepting promises based on future rewards rang in my head. "I still don't know why you want to do this for me. I mean, for nothing."

"I am a man who helps people reach their dreams." He cocked his head, raising his softly padded shoulders. "Does every good deed have to come with a dollar sign attached?"

"No, I guess not."

"All I want is your happiness."

"Yeah, I know. I was just making sure."

"So you will allow me to assist?"

"What about my parents? I mean, for right now, they don't have to know, right? You can do this stuff, like, behind the scenes?"

"Please tell your parents whatever you wish. But I won't breathe a word. In truth, you will never have to see me again."

I lifted one heel, then the other, dancing, trying to

stay warm. Then I squeezed my arms into a shrug. "Okay, man. Sure, why not? Knock yourself out. But, hey. I'm freezing my knucklebones off out here."

He extended his hand. "I am, as well."

We shook. As cold as my hands were, his fingers felt like frozen fish sticks. I couldn't let go fast enough. "Uh, Max, look, I better get going."

"Most certainly," he said. "Ah, but before you go, why don't you play your guitar?"

I couldn't think of a reason not to, so I jabbed the toe of my shoe between two side rails and let the old Gibson slide onto my knee. For some reason my hand loosened up right away as I fingerpicked the opening to "La Bamba." And it sounded out of this world, as if the guitar had an electric reverb unit installed, as if the whole sky were the dome of an opera house with finely engineered acoustics. "Whoa," I said.

Old Max burst into a big wheezy laugh. First time I'd ever heard him express any real emotion at all. But what an eerie throat note. If a lizard could laugh, I'm sure that's what it would sound like. The old dude breathed *in* when he laughed. It sounded like—like a strangled man trying to scream.

I walked home that night with a real rock-in-my-gut feeling that I'd either done something so ridiculous that I'd never want anyone to know about it or too freaky and bizarre to ever admit.

apple pie à la moody

I had a dead, zonked-out, dreamless sleep until about eight o'clock Saturday morning. Not much total time, but once my eyes popped open, that was it. I felt dread surge through me at the first thought of what had happened last night.

Maybe Max Lucero had no more power in the music biz than a flashlight battery would have trying to start a car. But what if he did? What if he could do half the things he said he could? I took a shower and got dressed holding on to one thought, hoping it would bring me some comfort. After my hideous performance last night, what did I have to lose? Not a red cent.

Visiting Glory was at the top of my agenda. I needed to find out how her game went and tell her I not only broke a leg, I think I broke my brain doing it. But I mainly hoped she could help lift me out of this "dreadful" mood I was in.

I didn't even call. I blasted off our porch and rode the front walkway to the little picket gate, which I jumped as my board rolled beneath it and emerged just in time for me to land on top and keep rolling. *Oh, man!* I had never done that before.

But I did not keep rolling. Instead, I screeched to a halt.

Snail trails across the sidewalk are so common, you barely notice them. But *these*. These were trails of an extremely uncommon variety. These were words, a shiny, slimy inscription gleaming from the sidewalk in front of my house:

UR SUM

TRUMPTER

Okay, so snails are not the best spellers in the world, or maybe they were hooked on phonics, but this low-tech IM was close enough for me to get the picture. I knelt to touch the tracks, to assure myself they were real.

Then I slowed my brain down a second and fell back to earth. My ears started burning so bad. I felt hot all over. Someone was messing with me. Someone was laughing at me right now. Under my hat brim, I casually spied up and down the street. Tran, maybe. Lil Lobo, most likely. Or even HoJo, the crazy pranksternmon. But someone had spent a lot of time herding a bunch of snails back and forth across the cement to make this stupid sign.

Still, no one appeared. No one came out cracking up from behind a hedge or dropping down from a tree.

Good, I thought. Then no one saw me get fooled. I kicked my board, got it square, and headed off to Glory's place. What I didn't even want to consider was that this could've been one of Max Lucero's confidence-building techniques.

I tapped my fingertips against her bedroom window. "Hey, it's me. You awake?"

Glory lifted the window open from the bottom. There was no screen, and I knelt down, so we were face to sleepy face. "Hey," she muttered in a low voice.

"How was your game?" I asked, as gently as I could.

"They killed me. They humiliated me."

I dropped my head. "I'm sorry. I bombed, too."

"You did?" She looked surprised. "That's not what Mom said. She said you might've been a little nervous, but it sounded like a good show."

"I don't know what happened, but it wasn't good. Cursed was more like it. I left the place thinking my career was over. That I'd ruined the best chance I would ever have."

"No, you didn't. Don't think that, Andy. You're way, way too good." She lifted her eyes, almost rolling them, and said, 'Okay, I have to tell you about my dream. It was only two seconds long. That's all I remember, but these people were listening to a radio, like on the seawall or somewhere, and they heard your music, and one guy says, 'That dude's some trumpeter.' And everybody just nods and they're all, 'Yeah. Right on.'"

My throat nearly closed up as I tried to swallow and breathe at the same time. I sat back on my shoes.

"What?" she asked.

I slowly rose up again, coming nearer. This was too crazy, so I just said, "Nothing. I wish it were true."

"What're you talking about? I took it as a good sign. That you're going to be a success." She gripped her forearms, crossing them on the windowsill, causing her comfy XL T-shirt to slip off her shoulder. "Hey, did you eat yet?"

"Eat?"

"Yeah, let's go get something. I want to get out of here." She pushed herself up. "Gimme a sec. I have to brush my hair."

In less than a minute, Glory had reappeared, sidesaddled her way through the window, and was standing next to me. Barefoot, ponytail, shorts, and a much tighter T-shirt. "Let's go to Stephanie's," she said, and led the way to the little bohemian strudel factory.

We sat at an outside table, sipping well-cinnamoned Mexican coffee, topped with whipped cream. My treat, since Dad had just paid me for the week. As soon as we were settled, and she'd broken off a piece of her apple strudel, Glory asked, "So what do we do now? Apparently, we're horrible without each other."

I decided to take a chance. "Have you ever heard of the Robert Johnson legend?"

Glory mm-mmed a "No" as she buried a forkful of strudel in her mouth.

"Well, he was an old blues musician who supposedly sold his soul to the devil for fame and fortune."

"Really? You can do that?" she said, rather cheerfully. "I like that idea. Has a softball player ever tried it?"

"No. I mean, I don't know." I sipped my coffee. Needed more sugar.

"Are you going to?" she asked.

"Well, no, I mean it's just a legend—as if you didn't know." I was sounding too serious, I could tell, so I forced a laugh—and sounded stupid. "But sometimes I think—I mean, what would you think if I did? If I sold out? Went all commercial and everything. Or like, if some guy offers to pull some strings for me, to sort of fast-track my career? Would that be wrong?"

"Are you really asking me? Or is this some kind of test?"

"No, I'm just—well, actually, yeah, you know, what would you think?"

"I'd say go for it." She cut off another piece of the pastry. "I mean, whatever. Is there some guy offering you this stuff or something?"

I hesitated, while twenty thoughts flashed across my mind. Right then, I wanted to tell her—I really thought I might—but I couldn't. I could not bring my-self to tell her the truth. I picked up a sugar packet from the bowl. "No, no, nothing like that."

"Too bad. My mom once told me about a Mexican healer—a *curador*—who could do stuff like that. Help people in business deals. They called him a root doc-tor because he used herbs and stuff."

"A root doctor?" I wondered if Grandpa would ap-prove of a guy like that—after all, I'd be remembering my roots.

"Yeah. He helped in romance, too. And lots of things."

"Did it really work?"

"For some people it did."

Could that be what Max was? A root doctor? No, I doubted it. I didn't think Max had any roots.

Glory brightened. "Hey, listen. Here's a plan. You sell your soul, get all rich and famous, and start a new fast-pitch professional softball team here in San Diego. We need one—and *I* could be their star pitcher."

I saw my way out of this and I took it. "Oh, so you're deciding to deal yourself into my evil bar-gain, huh?"

"I'm very clever."

"Yeah, well, you know what I'd tell the devil if he ever came to me with a big, fat offer like that? I'd say, 'I don't play for money, bubba. I play for Glory.'"

"You would not." She looked down at her plate and smiled.

"How do you know?" I gazed down Voltaire. "I'm very valiant. And I would do that before I'd try and hitch a ride on the back of *your* deal, Ms. Clever."

She ignored that to follow her own thought. "What would you really tell him? I mean, seriously. If you were offered the chance to have it all, if only you would trade in your soul?"

"I don't know." I kept going over and over my agreement with Max. It wasn't even close to that. It wasn't, right? So I played it clever. "Let me see if I can remember what I did last night."

"Oh, yeah, right."

"I *have* connections. I've got friends in low places." I casually sneaked a peek at her.

Her eyes were already waiting for mine. "That I know." She sounded ominous. "I saw you with them yesterday, at your party. And I think part of the reason I pitched so awful was because I was so upset."

"You were?" Make innocent face *now*, man. "Because of Madeline and everything?"

"Well, yeah." She looked at me over her cup of hot coffee.

I emptied one more sugar into mine. "I will never, I promise, miss another one of your games. All the way through the tournament. I totally promise."

"Good." She was noticeably relieved. She ate some more apple strudel, then stretched back against her chair.

I worked on my coffee and didn't mention any more clever deals. I wasn't so good at it anyway, since they seemed to backfire and leave me rather bummed. Although I did say, "But if you want me to, I'll go talk to Lil Lobo and Tran—about inciting the RaveRiders into doing treacherous things. Slap 'em around a few times. Give 'em something to think about."

She laughed. "Oh, thanks a lot. Yeah, sure, Andy the Enforcer. Except they're not the ones I'm worried about."

"Oh." I knew I should've shut up. "Right."

She slid her chair, so our knees were brushing, and leaned over. "Come here." She brought her face so close to mine, our noses almost touched. "I'm going to give you something to think about."

I submitted, hoping she'd do something to lift my mood. "Okay, but if you hurt me, I'm telling Lil Lobo."

She draped her arms over my shoulders, took a small breath, then said, "Don't ever leave me, okay?"

That was not what I had expected. Our eyes were so close, mine began bouncing off hers, from one to the other. Finally, I said, "I'm not leaving."

"Good," she whispered. "I'm glad."

After we settled back into our chairs again, I said, "The only thing I have lined up right now are your practices and games."

"Cool. We play two games next week, so remember. Monday and Wednesday, at five o'clock. The first one's up in Vista. The next one's down here. We practice on Tuesday."

"Right."

"The week after that, the tournaments begin, and we start playing for real."

I lifted both shoulders. "I'm all yours."

"You're supposed to say, 'I'll be there.' "

"Oh, yeah." I paused a bit. "But I didn't think it would sound as romantic."

She grinned just enough to make a dimple appear. "You're right," she said, locking her gaze on me. "It was much better."

I finished off my coffee, then stood. Stashing napkins into my paper cup, I began busing our table. As I tried to determine whether Glory was done finger-crumbing her plate, she looked up at me again. And I saw that certain secret glimmer. This time it said, "Well?"

I quit breathing. Slowly—and I mean like a feather falling—I leaned down, aiming my nose at her nose. At least, that was the last target I saw before I closed my eyes. But the first thing I felt was her hand on the back of my neck, pulling me closer. Her breath smelled like apple pie, warm and sweet.

And for the time being, I believe my mood had definitely been lifted.

After I left Glory's place, I rode home, got my horn, and skated back into town. Realizing that Max's secret was all mine—that I really had no one I could safely tell—sabotaged my momentary good mood. Blasting every banner, leaf, bike, and bird I saw along the way, I headed to South Beach, to the south side of the pier, where fewer people hung out. There, I figured, I could work on another new song rolling around my head, and I could be left alone.

Dropping down the steps from Niagara, I crossed under the pier, passed the happy campers who hung there, and made my way over to the small beach just below the cliffs. It was low tide, so I walked out into the tide pools, over the slippery black rocks. As I reached a strip of sand, I thought I recognized Glory's mom standing on the shoreline, letting the water roll over her feet.

Coming closer, I could see it was definitely her. With her hands tucked into the back pockets of her rolled-up jeans, the wind blowing her hair around, she stood facing the breakwater. After a few more steps around some rocks, I realized she was singing to the sea. I stood behind her, wanting to hear as much as I could before she turned around and saw me.

The song was that really cool Eagles tune, "Desperado." And when she ended, it was on the longest, most heartfelt enunciation of "desperado" I'd ever heard. It was so sad, I almost felt like crying.

Mrs. Martinez dipped her head, folded her arms across her chest, and made a tiny splash of a kick into the little lip of white water rushing her way. Then she turned and saw me.

"Oh, hi," she said, smiling big—that kind of embarrassed smile people put on when you catch them doing stuff they thought no one would notice.

"You have a beautiful voice."

"Oh!" She waved, then used the back of her hand to brush several strands of hair away from her cheek. "You don't have to say that."

"I'm being totally honest. I've always loved your voice. But the way you did that song was awesome."

"You're so sweet, Andresito. But—" Her voice turned weary. "—I haven't done any singing in so many years." She looked back at the ocean. "I don't know why I always seem to pick that song when I'm down here. If that man ever did show up again, I wouldn't have anything to do with him."

I realized she was probably talking about Glory's dad.

"I'm sorry," I said.

She sent me a sweet smile. "Oh, don't be. I guess I sing the song because I just wish it had been different back then."

"Glory never talks about him," I offered. "Her dad."

Mrs. Martinez walked closer. "She used to. I'd tell her stories. After a while, though, she'd heard everything I could remember. But you know something, Andy?" She waited until she could catch my eye, then went on. "I've never seen Glory as happy as she's been these past couple of weeks. You have done so much for that girl."

Me? "It's been totally mutual. Did Glory ever tell you how much she inspires me when I play music for her?"

"She did. She said that's what I was hearing the day I saw you two at the softball field."

"It's weird, but I think in a way we help each other reach a higher level."

"I think, in a way, you were made for each other." Then she glanced past me, over my shoulder. Quietly she said, "Just look at her."

I turned and watched Glory in her blue bikini with a towel around her hips making her way over the rocks and tide pools to join us. Looking up, grinning at us, looking down again for footing.

"And if she's happy," her mom added, "I'm over the moon."

"Andy!" Glory called, lifting a clump of wet hair

and trying to coax it into staying behind her ear. "Did Mom tell you? Olivia's coming back to OB Juan's tonight to talk about that weird reading she gave and what's been going on."

"Maybe we should be there," I answered.

She splashed up to us with her mouth open and her eyes slightly crossed. "Ya think?"

I slow-hammered her arm with my fist. "No, I don't think. Or I wouldn't be standing here taking sarcastic comments from you."

"Oh, quiet. You're coming tonight, right? Nine o'clock." She pointed her finger at my nose.

"I'll be there," I said.

Her finger continued toward me, and she flicked my cheek with her fingertips. "I'm there already." She zoomed her hand through an imaginary slice of sky. "I'm sitting there, growing my hair, looking all extra-ordinaire, waiting for you."

I just laughed, waving surrender at that line. Sometimes you have to know when to give up.

We occupied our usual booth at OB Juan's on Saturday night, though the girls' bench was now as squished as we were since Dakota, the team's shortstop, had joined us. Glory and Kayla had been working out at ShapeShifters, the gym Dakota's mom owned, and last week, Glory had introduced this tall, half-Polynesian, half–African American tenth grader with a burst of freckles across her nose to Tran. Now they had a little thing going.

Tonight he brought her flowers. Later tonight, Lil Lobo and I will kill him.

"Good evening, OBceans!" OB Juan's voice boomed over the P.A. "Lend me your ears." After the huge crowd cheered, he added, "Or at least twenty bucks—the drinks at this bar are really expensive!"

He got even more cheers for that line. "Okay, okay." He raised his hand. "Look, for those of you who don't know this little bit of history, my dad bought this place way back in the dark ages—yeah, that's right, the Reagan years." Rim shot. "And at that time the bar was called OB Good. True story. Bought it from a guy named Johnny." *Ba-dum-bump.* OB Juan sipped something from his coffee mug. "So then Pop gets what he figures is a million-dollar idea. He installs the very first karaoke machine. I tell you, it was so old, the thing didn't have a video monitor—it had an overhead projector. *Verdad.* Not making this up. And the overhead projector would've worked out just fine, except that, after two songs, my pop got so tired of holding that projector over his head that he dropped it on the floor and it shattered to pieces." Nice laugh. "Of course, that particular song was a smash hit." Big moans. "And speaking of smashed hits, here is OB's one and only fortune-teller to the stars, and the starfish, Olivia Olivetti!"

The drummer clanged away on the cymbals and kicked the bass, adding to the enthusiastic applause, as Olivia made her slow trek from the back of the barroom toward the stage.

"Silver and gold!" she said, as soon as she held the mic. "Silver and gold, dear people, cannot buy back the heat of a heart turned cold."

She sat on a wooden stool, closed her eyes, and took in a deep breath. "There is among us a cold, cold heart. And black clothes. Now, a young man has decided to step forth and satisfy the needs of this sad heart. But certain things are not as they appear. There is a shape-shifter among us."

"There are three of us," said Kayla, bumping elbows with Dakota. "And a lot more at your mom's gym."

"Shhh." I pressed a finger to my lips. What Olivia had just said fully drummed up my heartbeat.

"My dear people," she continued. "There is a trickster in OB, driving around in an SUV." She kept her eyes closed, saying nothing for a while, then added, "Looking for parking across the abyss. Please do not back up. Objects that you fear are closer than they appear. And don't leave town, in case we have any further questions. No, in case you lose your parking space." Olivia began shaking her head, her eyes still shut tight. 'Oh, it's all so garbled. Forget it, forget it. We never had this conversation! You're free to go."

Then she woke up, looking totally bewildered, to a

huge roar of laughter and a sea of bottles clinking in the air.

Glory and I looked at each other and shrugged. What did this have to do with us? It sounded like Olivia was talking about HoJo trying to park some Chevy Suburban in a "compact" zone. So, she stole the Holy Jokester's classic lines just for laughs? Was that it?

Or was it something else? The more I looked back at last night, the more I wished I could undo it all. I'd felt so bad ever since that moment. But nothing had really come from my little "Max pact." No instant benefits, like he said he could offer. In fact, today had been horrible from the time I woke up. My only happy times came when I was with Glory—and that wasn't because of Max. So maybe Olivia was delivering a message to me tonight. From Max. "Forget it. We never had this conversation." That the deal was off. And I was no longer standing on the edge of fire.

fire the bum

"**D**id you hear what she said?" asked Glory. "Was that supposed to help us? To save us from fire? Or crossing the big abyss?"

She and I had no chance at all to be alone and talk while we were hanging around OB Juan's that night, so as soon as I got home, I climbed out onto my roof ledge and called her.

"And what did she mean, Andy, about a cold, cold heart? Whose—mine? And so you just decided, out of pure goodness, to—whatever she said—to step forth and satisfy the needs of my poor, sad heart?"

"No, no, not at all, Glory. I've been thinking about it. Nothing she said had anything to do with us. I mean your heart these days isn't sad, right?"

"Yeah, true. I guess it could've all been her dumb routine. You know, with that parking bit and everything."

"I know. I don't think we should get too freaked."

"Okay," she said. And for a while neither one of us said anything. Until Glory whispered, "So, am I?"

"Are you what?"

"Your charity case? You did 'step forth' and rescue me, if you remember. On a day I was really sad."

"Well, yeah, of course I remember." Oh, no—I said it way too fast, with a real dose of irritation. I couldn't help it. But I tried to cover. "No, you're not a charity case. Not at all. You're just Glory." I hesitated, then followed a thought that had bolted in. "You're my heart on fire."

"I am?"

"Yeah, you are." I was back in control of myself.

"Really?"

I could hear her smile through the phone and I finally took a complete breath. "Sure," I told her. "I think I've known that for a while."

"What a sweet thing to say. That was the perfect thing to tell me."

"Thanks."

She took a breath. "Okay, so how's your deal with the devil working out?"

"My what?" That brought me to my feet. "Oh, that." I realized she was just trying to lighten things up. "Yeah, that was *nada*, baby. Nothing. Dude's a flop. The whole thing was a con. And really stupid on my part. I mean, look. Not one of my singles is at the top of the charts, and it's been a full day."

"Fire the bum."

"I think I will."

She gave a sweet squeal, then said, "Oh, hold on."

She covered the phone. "Andy, that's my mom. I gotta go. Thanks for making me feel better."

"Yeah, sure, call you tomorrow." I clicked the phone and sat back down, imagining her—what she was doing at that very moment. Would she be only half listening to her mom, eyes averted, so she—like me—could keep our conversation alive as long as possible? What do you think, Glory? I wondered. What if you're the fire in the heart of a guy who really does turn out to be a flop? I work and work for years and years and go nowhere. What if I end up being sad my whole life long and your fire for me burns out?

I stared out over the rooftops, toward the ocean. It was a pretty clear night. I found the Big Dipper, straight up. Nothing special. No trumpet. No new stars. Of course, I was not all that surprised. I just hoped one thing Max said was true. I hoped I would never have to see him again.

some gig wicked this way comes

Sunday was a crazy day. Something was not right. Soon as I woke up, I began writing tons of songs. The words, the melodies, the harmonies, the improv spots, just rolled out and kept on coming. With my guitar or without. At the keyboard or not. I'd been writing songs since I was thirteen, but never like this. Nonstop. My brain was in hyper mode, and it was draining me.

I was telling myself that I had finally hit my stride, creation-wise. That working on songs slowly and surely over the past few years was now paying off. I completely denied that Max Lucero could have anything to do with this flurry of furious writing.

And then the telephone rang.

"Andy? It's OB Juan. Listen, man, I need your help. We got a big cancellation just now for next Saturday night. Our headlining act is apparently booked at two different venues. And one of them is the L.A. County Jail."

"What?"

"Yeah, can you believe it?"

"But you said next Saturday night? My parents are playing for you that night."

"No, no, sorry. I didn't explain. I don't mean here at the bar. I'm talking about the OB Street Fair."

The *fair?* I thought. Oh, my gosh. The fair was huge. They'll have three stages up and down Newport with bands blasting all day and all night.

"Everyone heard you guys at the Farmers Market," OB Juan continued, "and you blew some minds. And you've had a little media lately, too. So how about it? We can't think of anyone else as good that we can line up on such short notice. You'd be center stage. Nine o'clock. Prime time. Can you help us out?"

This kind of stuff does not happen. No way was this a normal type deal. "Yeah," I said. "Sure. You kidding?" I almost expected him to say, "Yes."

But instead, he said, "Hey, thanks, bud. I owe you one. You guys'll be great. And you'll get a nice check, too. I'll go over the details with your folks. Sound all right?"

"Yeah, sure!"

I once touched an electric fence at a horse ranch. Sent a shock up my arm that buzzed me from my elbow to my teeth. The shock OB Juan just gave me carried ten times the voltage, and I wasn't going to be able to simply let go of it and walk away. I was going to be stunned for quite a while.

A break like this was *gigante*. Wicked *gigante*.

By Sunday night, it became obvious something was seriously weird. I lay in bed with songs still churning inside my head. Notes, words, chord progressions, everything. That's when I knew I must've really done something powerful that foggy night and, most likely, dangerous and stupid. And it was out of my control.

"What do I do now, *Abuelito*? I'm in a mess."

Instantly, that plea became a song. "What do I do, / what did I do, / what do I do now?" Horn blast. "I confess I'm in / this mess I'm in. / How do I get out?" Guitar solo. *Wah-wah*. It was crazy.

I got up and walked down the hall. "Dad," I said, waving at him in his music library, where he was at his desk, his headphones on. Looked like he'd been working on breaking down the words and music to a song he was learning. "I have to talk to you."

"Sure, Andrés." He removed the headphones and placed his pencil on his pad. I could tell by his cool manner in using my formal name, the way he spun his chair and pointed to another, he was not expecting anything big.

I cleared my throat and began. "On Friday night, after the radio show, I couldn't sleep at all. So I got up and took my guitar out onto the pier. At the—at the part where the T forms. Where it makes kind of a crossroads?"

Dad eased into a grin. "What were you thinking,

mijo? That *el diablo* would come by and tune your guitar?"

"Dad, there *is* this strange guy. And he, like, shows up at all these different times and places. So I'm just standing out there, writing and thinking, resting my elbows on the rail, and all of a sudden I look up and see this old dude hunched over my guitar."

"He was there?"

"*Yeah.*"

"Well, you know, it's a free country. It's a free pier. So what'd the guy do?"

"It's not what *he* did, really. It's what I did. He tells me he has all these music connections and wants to help me out and everything, and—and we shook hands and I think I sold him my soul."

Dad leaned forward with his arms on his knees "You did not sell anyone your soul. Okay, *mijo*? No one can do that. No one can buy it from you. That's just an old legend, all right? Now look, who is this guy? What do you know about him?"

"Not much. He's Max Lucero and he's old and kind of bent over and he dresses like he's some immigrant from an old village in Europe. He has a cane and wears a black suit and hat. But he says he can make things happen."

"And where else have you seen him?"

"All over the place. He gets around a lot. And Glory even dreamed about him."

Dad held up a hand. "Okay, hold on. Look, I don't doubt what you're telling me. I go on that pier myself sometimes, late at night. It's a good place to go for the reasons you did—to sort things out. And I see some strange characters out there, too. Were there other people around?"

"No. Well, I don't know, maybe. It was kind of foggy."

For the first time, Dad frowned. "Andrés. What were you thinking? No one around. Hard to see anything. You know better than that."

"I know. I'm sorry—I wasn't exactly thinking too clearly. But you know, I messed up so bad on 'The Lounge' that night, and this little guy had been telling me how much a good promoter could do for my career, that he could make things happen. And look, now this big, huge gig comes my way from out of nowhere, and . . ."

"Do what for your career? You're fifteen years old."

"So? Look at Wynton Marsalis. And tons of other guys. There's guys out there who didn't even finish high school because they got cranking on stuff, making money and everything. There are lots of professionals who started at my age."

"Okay, we're off the subject here." Dad leaned back in his chair and I leaned forward. "We need to find out some more about this Max Lucero, who he is, what he's all about. And he says he'll show you what he can do? Okay, let him. You didn't sign anything, right?"

"No."

"Wouldn't be legal anyway. You're underage. How much did he want?"

"Nothing. That's the weird part."

Finally, Dad's face eased and relaxed. A small grin appeared. 'I wouldn't worry too much about it, bud. Next time you see him, call me, okay? Introduce us. That's the right thing to do. Meanwhile, try to remember something. You, Andy, have worked extremely hard for everything that's come your way. No one has given you anything. And they sure didn't buy anything from you." He stood up and wrapped his arm—the crook of his elbow—around my neck, pulling me toward him. "And besides, you *are* too young for one thing. You're too young to become a legend."

Dad was so cool that night. No big bad music biz lecture. No jumping on me about the vision I had of making a big splash in the music world. He just brought me what I needed—tons of comfort.

"Okay,' I said. "Thanks, Dad."

He knuckled my head a little. "Get a good sleep, *mijo*."

"I will"

let the games begin

Monday morning, I woke up not feeling much better, despite how I felt as I went to sleep. Sure, I was excited about the street fair. After I told Lil Lobo and Tran, it really sank in how awesome it was to land that gig. But it still felt like something was wrong inside. And it was strange the way words and music just kept spilling out of my brain. I took my trumpet and sat on the Sunset Cliffs, above the ocean, and played into the wind, writing some more.

Verses for songs that I didn't even know about, along with compositions and orchestrations, filled my notebook. I looked forward to Glory's game today, just for the chance to break out of this songwriting frenzy. And it was *très* cool telling her about the new gig. We just hugged and swayed. Being with Glory still settled me down a lot.

I rode up with some of the players, and when we arrived at the ballpark in Vista that afternoon, Glory, Kayla, and I headed down to the bullpen.

"Where do you want me to be?" I asked. "In the

stands, along the fence, in that eucalyptus tree over there?"

"In the stands, like you've been doing in practice."

"Okay," I said. "You look good. I mean, like you're a really good pitcher."

"Just go. I know what I look like." Oohh, she was a bit touchy.

From the stands, I watched as her whole team stood in front of the dugout in a chorus line, dancing to Glory's CD on a boombox. They had this cool routine worked out—kicks, twirls, and claps—all built around the tunes I'd recorded for Glory. I decided to call it "Beauty and the Geeks," but it was fun.

Since the RaveRiders were visiting, they came to bat first. Glory, however, was not in the lineup. Besides the fact that she was not a very good hitter—as opposed to Kayla, who was batting over .400—today she was pitching, so it was natural for the coach to put in a DH, or designated hitter, for her. Glory could then fully concentrate on her pitching. These were just a few of the things I'd learned hearing all this baseball talk

In the first inning, Glory was a little too anxious rushing her motion, using hyper windups and not taking enough time between pitches. Half of them hit the dirt before they even crossed the plate. For some reason, she just wasn't hearing me.

After walking the first two batters, I saw her take a

deep breath and turn my way. She raised her shoulders and then released them.

I began snapping my fingers to the beat she needed to get back to. I thought that maybe she needed to *see* the rhythm that she was too tense to hear. It was a good guess. She struck out the next hitter, and the girl after her bounced the ball to Dakota at short, who started a nice double play.

Glory coasted after that. She would signal me with her eyes—just a glance—whenever she needed me to calm her, to remind her of her rhythm once again. But beyond that, she could pitch well without the music for several batters in a row. In the last inning, though, she may have become too predictable in the selection of her pitches. The first two hitters swung at her first pitch, and they each got singles.

Because their lead was only 2–0, Kayla called time and jogged out to the pitcher's circle. She said a few things to Glory, they both nodded, and Kayla left. Glory didn't actually throw another strike for the rest of the inning—but her pitches were close and so tempting that the hitters could not keep themselves from trying to connect. They connected all right, but only managed two pop-ups—one fair, one foul—and a dribbler back to Glory, which she threw to first for the final out of the game.

Funny, but I hated to see the game end. It only

meant going back home and getting a little more agitated, worried, frenzied, or blue. I just wished I knew what was going on.

When she, Kayla, and Dakota showed up at the studio on Tuesday afternoon, Glory had an ice pack wrapped around her shoulder.

"Were you pitching today?" I asked.

"No, it just tightened up on me. Besides, doesn't it make me look extra cool?"

"Ha, ha," said Dakota, who was first to realize Glory was trying to make a joke about the ice. "Too bad it also makes you look extra doofus."

Glory only grinned and relaxed into the soft chair. "Play us something new, you guys."

"Don't say that," said Tran. "Andy will whip out a song on the spot, then make us learn it."

"I could if I wanted to."

Lil Lobo didn't let that happen. "Listen to this one," he said. "It's called 'Degrees of Love.'"

He rat-a-tatted his tinpan drum, setting a quicker, more syncopated beat than we'd been using, with more of a reggae flavor. Tran fell in next, bass strings only. Steel drum. Bass guitar. Then me. I blew a long, low, sultry note, ending the measure in melodic triplets.

After that Tran's guitar lit up the place, and we were rolling. It turned out to be our best rendition yet.

Because of Glory? Well, yeah, and probably because of Kayla and Dakota, who totally grooved on it, dancing with their eyes closed.

But it did make me realize something I hadn't seen before. A song's journey, I realized, is not complete until it reaches an audience, and they respond. I could see that now, and it was all I really wanted to do with my music. To complete that circle. In fact, it had now become something I craved.

I showed up early for Glory's second game on Wednesday. This one was back at Robb Field, so I hoped that would also give her a little home field advantage. But when I arrived, Glory was not even ready to loosen up. She sat up in the bleachers, talking to some reporters.

At first, I thought they'd come by to get a few pictures and quotes for a feature story about the wide range of upcoming Fourth of July weekend activities, like they always do.

I quickly found out they were more interested in Glory, the girl who pitches to music. There was a local radio sportscaster, a sportswriter, and a reporter from the weekly lifestyle section, talking to the girls and shooting pictures. Eventually they followed us down to the bullpen to get some action shots. I didn't mind. It was actually kind of cool.

And this time when the game started, the fans

joined in as I played the cheer routine. That was better than I could have ever imagined. With every pitch, moms and dads, little sisters, even brothers, all joined in, clapping, stomping, or doing something to the beat.

And whether it was because of my trumpet or the cheering fans or all the media attention she was getting, I'll never know. But that was the day Glory pitched a perfect game. Seven innings. Twenty-one batters came to the plate. And twenty-one straight outs were recorded, including twelve strikeouts by Glory. It took me a moment to stop and fully realize that not a single player from the other team had even made it to first base.

In softball, I learned that pitchers tended to dominate, so it wasn't all that unusual to see a no-hitter or even a perfect game. But this team—the one she beat—had not lost a game in two months. In fact, they were considered one of the top travelball teams in the state.

Suddenly, I realized there was a new star in the sky. Not me, but instead a bright, huge, overpowering softball pitcher was shouldering her way into the cosmos.

PART III *a vortex of things unseen*

This rivermouth town has been a crossroads town since the river was a stream. A vortex of things hoped for, *mis amigos,* a conjunction of things unseen.

From the days when the OB Spaceman sold tickets for a rocket trip to far-off cosmic hotels, to the day the great OBcean lefty, a boomer named David Wells, pitched a perfect game in Yankee Stadium, where his spirit to this day dwells, OB has been a crossroads town.

Never underestimate, *mijo,* the powers of this place, nor forget that they can reach from the trails of snails to outer space.

just don't jump to any delusions

"**Y**ou were incredible today," I told Glory, as she, Kayla, Lil Lobo, and I held down a booth at OB Juan's, macking out on chicken quesadillas, beer-battered french fries, and Cokes. "I keep thinking about it."

"I know," she said. "It was great, wasn't it? Especially in front of all those reporters."

"Give me a break, you guys." Lil Lobo dropped his head. He was fully acting out a role, with his huge pair of old-man wraparound shades, looking like some Delta bluesman, like Ray Charles or somebody. "People already think you're the little darlings of the town. You don't have to keep reminding yourselves."

"Yeah," said Kayla, "you make it sound like there were only two players on the winning team today. Not even a catcher, who was calling every single pitch, may I remind you."

"Tell it, sister," said Lil Lobo. *"Verdad,* that."

Before Glory or I could sting them back, we heard OB Juan's voice come over the P.A. system, asking us all to lend him our ears.

"Thank you, *mis amigos*, for coming tonight. Let me start off by saying, you all know that Cito and Jayney Ramos and their band, Soy Capitán, are a permanent feature here each week. But now I want to announce that the next generation, their son Andy Ramos, and his boys, Tran and Lil Lobo, are preparing to launch their band, FuChar Skool, this Sunday, center stage, at the world famous OB Street Fair and Chili Cook-Off. Catch them if you can. It will be worth it. If not for the sake of this band, then for the sake of your own peace of mind. And now, please put your hands together for *Soy Capitán!*"

That was weird. Hearing my name over a sound system, my parents', too, and all in the context of promoting me and the guys' first professional gig.

"You guys are famous!" Kayla was almost breathless. She squeezed her eyes together with a smile of pure delight. "That is so cool."

"And," said Glory, "we can say we knew you when."

Lil Lobo continued with the head-bob deal. "Get used to it, baby. It's only gonna get better."

Even I had to punch him after saying that. "Oh, yeah?" I asked. "What do you mean *better*? Are we getting a new drummer?"

He pointed at me. "Cruel. You are insensitive and egocentrific." But never one to miss an opportunity, he added, "Kayla, will you please come over and put your arm around me? I am full of pain and misery."

"You are half right," I said. "But I got another word besides *pain*."

He smiled, but by then Kayla had already bopped around to our side, changing places with me, and the reality of our lives shifted once again.

"Hey, you guys," I said, after we were settled. "I haven't heard my parents play in a long time. They have a new drummer, and—get this—Mom's been working on a Britney Spears song."

Lil Lobo was all over that. "Oh, you lie like—"

I waved my hand. "No, no, man. No joke. They do this full-on punk version of 'Oops! . . . I Did It Again,' and my dad does this boom-dawg Mike Watt bassline while Mom screeches it like—I don't know—like Courtney Love or somebody. I heard them practicing."

Lil Lobo grabbed my arm. "Dude, look at me."

I did.

"We have to learn that version," he said, stabbing his finger at me. "And we'll get Tran to sing it. See, dude, that'll be loverboy's next gift to Dakota."

Glory slammed her hand on the table. "Oh, yeah. Britney punk. Just what every girl wants to hear."

Lil Lobo bongoed the table. "We aim to please," he said, but quickly turned his attention to my mom and dad.

However, Soy Capitán opened with one of their usuals, obviously saving "Oops!" for a later, and "looser," crowd.

Still, they rocked. Mom was belting out "Hand in My Pocket," warming up the crowd for the night, as the temp at our table rose way above normal and stayed there all night long.

"Andy," said Glory over the phone the next morning. "It's worse."

"What is?" I'd come to the studio early to help Dad set up for several other bands who, like FuChar Skool, were fine-tuning for the Street Fair in four days. Mom must've told Glory, so she could reach me.

"My arm. My shoulder really hurts. I've iced it and everything, but it's worse than it was after the game. Maybe I slept on it funny or something."

"Did you call your coach?" Dad handed me several additional lengths of guitar cable to run to the front of the room.

"No, but Kayla says I should go see a trainer she knows."

"Well, you've been pitching a lot." I used my knees to push the couch away from the wall and stepped on the remnants of a red-chili-potato-and-steak burrito that Lil Lobo had tossed at me, like, a week ago. I opened the door and shoe-slapped the dusty chunk out into the alley for the crows to devour.

"Andy, I've pitched fifteen innings in one day before. And I've never had shoulder problems."

I could not find the power box for the speaker

monitors, so I decided to unplug the floor lamp and plug in a surge protector. "So then, maybe this is nothing. When do you see the trainer?"

"I don't know." She hesitated. "I don't want to go."

"Why not?" I was on the hot floor, looking under the surfboard coffee table and all along the baseboard for an extra surge-protector strip laying around. We didn't use toolboxes or anything. Dad and I liked things out in the open so we could find them.

"Because our first road trip is next week. We're going to Santa Barbara for four days, and I don't want to miss it."

I sat up on my knees. The whole room was hot. "I can't go to Santa Barbara with you."

"I know. That's why I never said anything about it. But I'll be ready by then. So why get a sports trainer involved, who'll tell me to rest up for a week or two, just to be on the safe side?"

"That'd be an unusual side for you to be on, wouldn't it?" On my belly again, I saw a dim red glow near the forty-roll bundle of toilet paper spilling out of a bag beneath the card table across the room.

"You know what I mean," she said.

I totally did, since I was someone who'd also spent my whole life listening to my heart, and not my head, when it came to stuff like this. "Okay, so what kind of workout will you do today?" I started to crawl. As I reached the power strip, I was sweating like crazy.

"Light weights. Crunches. Leg work in the ocean. But no swimming. And I won't throw. So that means you are free to go. I can do all that on my own."

"Okay, that's cool." Even though it had no surge guard, the strip did have an open receptacle, so to save time, I plugged the monitor amp into it, then crawled out backward from beneath the table. "We're practicing in Tran's garage today, because the studio's so booked, and we seriously need to do some marathon session work, since Sunday is coming right up."

"I won't bug you. Call me if you need me."

"Bug me if you need *me*. Okay?" Somewhere, I smelled smoke.

She assured me she would and hung up.

Realizing what I'd done, I dove back in, lunging for the smoldering power strip, just as the whole studio went dark.

FuChar Skool rehearsed until ten o'clock that night, and we picked it up again on Friday. Dad had the circuit breaker problem fixed fairly quickly at the studio, and I told him I'd pay for everything he needed. First time I'd ever said anything like that to him. But I knew that soon I'd be raking in major coin. All part of being the next major talent to grace musicland, I figured. It was starting to taste pretty good.

I didn't hear from Glory all Friday, but I figured no news was okay for the time being, since I'd noticed that a power surge of a different sort had taken place. I could now play deep, inspired music without her presence. I had no idea how—or when—it had happened, but I also attributed it to the higher level of fame I was now starting to visualize as being right around the corner.

By Saturday, I began feeling really guilty. The band's work was going great, but we had pretty much excluded girls from the picture, so that it would. I mean, focus-wise. So I called her.

"Glory, it's me," I said to her voicemail. "A distant memory from out of your past. Howzit? Call me. Bug me. 'Bye."

She didn't call. When I finally reached her Sunday morning, she started crying as soon as I said, "Morning, Glory."

"The trainer thinks it's a torn rotator cuff. She wants me to have an MRI, but it's so expensive. We don't have insurance." I started to say something, but she talked right over me. "Plus, I know she's wrong. I have a complete shoulder workout I do that builds up and strengthens that whole region. And I've been doing my backstroke routine for over a year. If anything, it's just a strained muscle. Ever since I started pitching to your music, my mechanics have changed. Not much, but I'm using slightly different muscles. So that could be it."

"That s all it is, you think? Rest will help, right?"

"Well, yeah. That's why I've been crying for two days. I really wanted to pitch in Santa Barbara, since the coach from Cal Berkeley will be there. Now I might not even be ready for the Firecracker Tournament down here next Friday."

"Wait, don't jump to any conclusions yet. Look, you coming to our gig today?" First things first.

"I was planning on it."

"Good. Because I will totally lift you up, I promise." Plus, I needed to show her how much I could stream the extremes on my own now, all night long, if I needed to.

She didn't say anything for a moment. I heard a quiet sob. "That's what I need, Andy."

"Yeah, yeah," I said. "Me, too."

I had never seen so many people in the street before. Any street. I mean, you couldn't scratch your back without elbowing two people behind you. At the weekly Farmers Market the crowd was mostly locals. But this—the annual OB Street Fair—attracts thousands from all over Southern California. There were three stages, tents everywhere, and chili smoke filling the air. By the time we jumped up onstage, the sun had gone down and the serious music lovers were out in force. And man, we rocked.

The salsa hip-hop tunes ripped. People really zoned into the new sound. On "Fundamental Fusion," I climbed the scales a couple of octaves, sat up there, jamming a while, then came back down and into my basement, low as I could go, slowing the rhythm by elongating the notes, then I took it on home.

It was blues-infested jazz on a Latin beat, and, man, it filled the street. Whole lotta shaka-shaka going on. The jazz trumpet intro to "Arm's Reach Away" seemed to, almost eerily, take their breath away. They got so quiet, until Lil Lobo's steel drum kicked in. Then it was a NASCAR crash scene and bodies flying everywhere. Up onstage, too. I was actually having fun—at least for a while.

That lasted until the moment I noticed Glory's arm was in a sling. And I saw the distance in her eyes. Oh, dude, that was not what I needed. We were halfway through our set before Glory and the rest of the Ravers could muscle their way to the front. For the rest of the set, I just had to ignore her or else I knew I'd slip into a funk.

Afterward, she and I got separated by the crowd. While the band exited backstage, Glory and her friends got trapped in front. But as soon as I could, I called her cell.

"What'd you think, baby? What'd you think?"

"I liked it," she said, softly.

"You did, huh?" Not much energy from her tonight. "You okay? What's with the sling?"

"I'm miserable. It's just been bad news on top of

bad news. I'll definitely miss the Santa Barbara tournament."

"What a bummer. So it's more serious than you thought?"

"Actually, no one even knows what it is. Maggie's dad's a doctor and he gave me the sling. But he said it wasn't the rotator cuff. He thinks it's just overuse because it sort of comes and goes."

"It does?"

"Yeah, it was fine again last Wednesday."

Wednesday, I remembered, was the day she—and I—pitched a perfect game. The day all the local media were there. At that instant, I began to realize that Glory needed me more than I needed her. The improv spark, the fiery bulb that had lit so many outrageous musical ideas over the past week—ever since Max and I had shaken hands—was now, I realized, burning on its own. And I remembered the distance I'd seen in her eyes tonight. Was that a sign of things to come? Were we drifting apart?

"So, where are you now?" I asked. "Let's meet up."

"I can't. We're leaving early tomorrow for Santa Barbara, so I'm on my way home to pack. I'll be going up just to help keep stats and stuff."

"When'll you be back?"

"By Thursday. The Firecracker thing starts Friday afternoon, and I *have* to be ready for it."

"You will. I'll make sure. Just go easy, okay?" We were drifting. I could feel it. "Hey, I'll miss you."

"Thanks, me, too."

"But don't worry," I said. "When your firecracker deal starts, I'll definitely be there."

"Yeah?" she said. "Well, I'm there already. I've got my arm in a sling and I'm—I'm starting to sing. The blues. Waiting—for yous!"

Ah, man, it felt good to laugh. "Glory! You are an amazing chick, as far as chicks go."

"Shut up."

"Have a good trip."

"Thanks."

"And, uh . . ." Realizing I was about to say good-bye for four days, realizing that even though she was leaving, I was the one who felt like moving on, I wanted to say something huge and heartfelt. I knew I could've said any dumb thing. But I went for the grand prize. ". . . I love you."

I had never said those words in such a way to anyone before, and it panicked me a little. After several moments, she finally said, "That is the best news I've heard in a long time."

beware of all gigs that require new clothes

Dad officially became the manager of FuChar Skool the day after the OB Street Fair. We needed somebody. Fast.

OB Juan had referred two calls to our house before noon, each one having to do with a booking at a major music club, as long as we passed an audition. The audition would be our performance at the Fourth of July concert we'd be giving from the balcony of the Dharma Center on Newport next Sunday. What Fourth of July concert? Well, apparently there was another last-minute cancellation, and no one else to call on such short notice except us. Sound suspicious? I quit thinking about it.

Oh, and how did these booking agents hear about us? You got me. The Holy Jokester's standard phrase, "The night has a thousand eyes," was the best answer anyone could come up with.

Dad had never heard of anything like this. The calls coming in were from L.A. clubs owned by record companies. And Dad said it worked pretty much like this. First, they need to hear a buzz about you. Our buzz must have been by ESP—or smoke signal. Anyway, then they actually fly in to see a show. If they like what they see, they book you into one of their dance clubs. And if you shoot out the lights and the crowd goes wild for a certain period of time—say a couple of weeks or months—it's a pretty sure bet that they'll offer you a recording contract.

Despite all the good news, I still couldn't shake the restless, uneasy feeling that seemed to creep up anytime I was alone.

"This is huge," said Lil Lobo. "This ain't no long shot by a long shot." We sat in Dad's studio, soaking in the news. Lil Lobo had none of his usual swagger, no show-dawg machoisms, no tongue-in-cheek overspeak. He was dead serious, and it scared me a little to hear him be in so much awe of our new situation. "We're on the *verge*, dudes, of reaching out and grabbing that billion-mile-away star—and the moon with it."

"Dude," I said, agreeing with his assessment.

Tran helped put it all into perspective. "Do we have to buy new clothes and learn dance steps and everything?"

"You have to learn your songs," said Dad, "perfectly. Your musicianship needs to be flawless. But, on the other hand, you are entertainers. So, yeah, man, you'll also need to put on a show."

"But it's huge," said Lil Lobo. "I mean, this is humongous."

"It's cool," said Dad, definitely trying to downplay

things, hoping Lil Lobo would get back to being himself. My dad knew as well as I did that if Lil Lobo went catatonic on us, it would *not* be good.

Dad was going to say more, but his phone rang, and once he started talking, we could all tell it was another business call regarding the FuChar.

For the rest of the week, the plan was pure, nonstop rehearsal. Grandpa used to talk about how I had to immerse myself into music, and I always thought I knew what he'd meant. Man, I didn't know jack. I barely knew Jill, as Mom would say.

This was immersion. And I had the sneaky feeling that one day I'd look back and laugh that I thought *this* was immersion, once I really learned what that trip was all about.

Then on top of it all, Glory showed up on Thursday night, back from her road trip, looking peppy and perky and slingless. "Well," I asked, "how's your arm?" I was sure I didn't sound as enthusiastic as she looked.

"So much better. Dakota's mom did acupuncture on me the whole trip. And she gave me these special herbs for muscle repair. They really worked."

I truly hoped the herbs and stuff had helped, because with the way things had been happening—and unhappening—around here, with no noticeable connection to the world as I knew it—as I *used to* know it—I was not convinced a little "outside force" had not been used on her.

"Right on," I said. "So can you pitch?"

"I think so. I'll see tomorrow. But can you—can you be there? It starts at five o'clock."

Oh, her eyes—they were puppy-dog-in-a-box unfair. "You know I already promised I would."

"I know, but—"

I gave her a narrowed glance. "Lil Lobo? What do you think, man? Can I be there?"

He spoke in a slow, somber voice. "Glory, he is already there, angel. Trust in the force."

Did Marty Rojas just say that? I smiled, leaning forward, and said, "Yeah, the force. Because, baby, I'm there, like a flying horse."

shoulder-tattooed soccer moms
and deep revelation

I have to say, the people I saw heading toward the Firecracker Tournament ballfields on Friday afternoon were the strangest mix of softball fans I'd ever seen.

"They're all coming to see Glory, right?" asked Tran, as we crossed the Robb Field parking lot.

"And our boy Ramos, here," said Lil Lobo. "The dynamic duo."

I gazed over the wave of bearded guys with headbands and earrings, shoulder-tattooed soccer moms with beach chairs and coolers, yuppie parents from the other teams, and Green Party cats, walking backward and handing out flyers on how a sewage spill is no day at the beach. Whole families and stragglers alike, scores of people, walked along, beaming in the sunlight with basically every skin color you can imagine, including biker-bar white.

"I doubt anyone's here because of me," I said. "These people are softball fanatics. But in a few months they'll pack this place from Sk8 Park to Thee Bungalow just to hear me play." I pointed straight ahead. "I'll be on top of that backstop, baby, where the legend began."

"Quiet your riot, *carnal*," said Lil Lobo. "You're getting all hyped over your own imaginary hype."

"Oh, yeah?" Before I could remind him how zombastic he'd turned a few days ago, a woman walked up to us. She looked like a college student with an I-do-mean-business attitude.

"Andy Ramos?" she asked.

"Yeah."

"Hope Cassidy, with the *San Diego Union-Tribune*. May I ask a few questions?"

"Sure."

Holding a silver palm-sized recorder near her mouth, she started. "How did you discover that your music could get Glory to perform at such a high level?"

She thrust the recorder toward me. "Well, um—tough question." I rubbed my neck. "I think my first clue was when I saw it happen."

"But did you have any idea ahead of time? When did it occur to you to try this unusual technique?"

"Well, it never actually occurred to me. When I first tried it, I was pretty much just goofing around." And I decided to goof around with this way-too-serious reporter. "Then after I saw what was happening, from that point on, I was more or less totally trying to impress a pretty girl. Purely for the sake of romance motivated by—you know—impure thoughts and physical desire. Is my mother going to read this?"

"That would be up to her, I suppose. The story'll run in tomorrow's edition."

"Of the *OB Rag*?" I said, ragging her.

"No, the *Union-Trib*."

"Okay, then, I'm safe. You can use that last quote, if you wish."

"Yes, right." She checked her notes. "I guess that's it. Thank you for your time." The poor lady then took off toward the RaveRiders' dugout.

"She should've asked me about you and Glory," said Lil Lobo, as we watched her scurry away. "I would've told her the truth."

"Which is?"

"Horn players are always horny."

"See, that's why nobody interviews you, dawg. They don't want obvious answers. They want depth. They want revelation."

Lil Lobo nodded. "I'll try to remember that." He waited a beat. "I could take off my shirt. That's revealing."

"Dude, quiet. You are so shallow."

He shouldered me sideways; I tripped, but caught myself, and we continued on our way.

The atmosphere at the ballfield burned electric, a lot like that day about a month ago when I first played for Glory and all those out-of-town teams were beehiving around the complex. Except there were more teams this time. At least eight, Glory had said.

Several games with three o'clock start times were halfway over already. The RaveRiders occupied a vacant field, going through their stretches and yelling at each other as if they were screaming out their butterflies. I left Tran and Lil Lobo and found Glory with Kayla and their coach way down at the bullpen.

Glory threw a pitch. "Any pain?" asked Becca.

"No. Feels good."

"Stay within yourself."

"I will."

I watched a while longer, then asked, "Really? No pain at all?"

"Start playing," said Glory. "Game starts in half an hour."

The game became a concert. I should've known, bringing a drummer along, that I wasn't going to perform alone. Especially when it's my shirtless friend here, Shy Boy Willie Brown, with his black T-shirt flipped over his head and down his back, like a nun's habit. But I didn't expect the fan-dancing in the stands that Lil Lobo inspired simply by using two sticks on a bleacher seat. People were even coming up asking us to play requests. I think if I never play Queen's "We Will Rock You" again, it will still be too soon. But the percussions were cool, and it kept me from getting bored.

Lil Lobo and I actually played more during the breaks between batters than the short bursts we did for Glory's pitching. Didn't bother her a bit. Maybe even helped, though she was fully inside herself, centered the entire time on the next pitch and Kayla's mitt.

She had lost some speed, I could tell, from taking the week off maybe—or from holding back due to a still-tender arm. But that also seemed to help her curve and drop balls. They were breaking like waves over the seawall.

In the second inning, the lead-off batter for the Escondido team struck out on an outside drop. The next hitter, though, slapped the same pitch straight down, sending a high chopper back toward Glory. She got her glove on it, but the ball bubbled out, and Glory could make no play at first.

The following batter, a lefty, drove a low, outside fastball through the infield, just past Dakota's outstretched glove, and it rolled all the way to the left field fence, scoring the runner on first.

Glory stepped back and stared at her feet. She did not seem real thrilled. Then she tapped the ball into her glove a few times. I could also detect a slight bounce in one knee, setting a beat that was just a tick slower than the one we'd worked out before the game.

I was on it. Lifting my trumpet, I rattled something useless to get her attention, then I put the new tempo to her rhythm song. Lil Lobo followed my lead.

Glory got set, came forward like a charging horse,

and released a belt-high riser just outside the strike zone that the other girl waved her bat at. Totally fooled.

Glory followed up with a fastball at the knees on the inside corner, which was called a strike. I knew enough by then to know the batter was being set up for the killer pitch, a drop-curve that broke in toward her hands. Even if she'd known the pitch was coming, I doubt the hitter would have fared any better. Her timing was so far off, she stepped way too soon, then made a last-ditch swipe at the pitch, missing it completely.

A slow roller to first finished the inning, leaving an Escondido runner on second and the RaveRiders down, 1–0.

Between defensive outings, I stood at the back of the dugout, where the team energy was spiking. "Nice recovery," I told Glory.

"Thanks. You, too."

Dakota walked up saying, "Glory, I need to know the pitches, okay? I need to know what's coming, so I'm leaning the right way. I could've got that stupid roller through the hole."

"That's my fault," said Kayla. "I'll slow down and make sure you can see the signs."

"Don't worry," said Glory. "There won't be any more seeing-eye singles. I got my rhythm now."

And that was true. Three straight hits in the third put the RaveRiders on top, 2–1, and forty-five minutes later, that became the final score.

After the girls jumped, screamed, hugged, and generally celebrated, I waited for one thing. The look in Glory's eyes. I needed to see if the pain in her shoulder had returned. She caught me staring and smiled, but it was too late. Just before that, she'd shifted her shoulder to check for pain, and I'd seen the dip of her eyebrow, the tension in her forehead, her eyes wincing.

"Don't worry," she said, walking up. "It's under control."

"Okay, but don't hurt yourself. It's not worth it."

"How do you know what this is worth to me?" she snapped. "You're on the verge of a recording contract. Everything's going your way. I'm fighting to get a little bit of notice in a state full of great softball pitchers. How could you possibly know what this means to me?"

"Hey, I'm only saying." Oh great, I thought. She turns on me after everything I've done. Is she actually blaming her sore arm on me? Or is she just jealous?

fast-pitch
rocket science

During the first game Saturday morning, my higher-level trumpeting worked better than ever. I was playing solo—it being way too early for Lil Lobo—but all I had to do was get Glory revved up, and the fans took care of the rest. Once I worked out her rhythm of the day, that was it, basically. The crowd kept the beat without me, and Glory responded.

The only baserunners for the other team came in the second and fourth innings. The first one hit a high hopper that Dakota stayed back on. In a flash, the batter had crossed first base a half step ahead of the sharp throw. The other runner walked, on a very close pitch. But nobody scored, and Glory's team beat the girls from Mission Viejo, 2–0.

The next game started fifteen minutes later, on a neighboring field. The tournament director wanted to keep the games running in rapid succession so there was never a big lull in the tourney.

That was great for me. The faster the games moved along, the sooner I could get back to Lil Lobo and Tran and work some more on our set for tomorrow. I hated to say it, but this softball stuff was starting to become a distraction.

The second game of the day, however, was more challenging, and Glory needed more help with her "rhythm-ology" than before. Though her pitching motion was the same for every kind of pitch she threw—drop-curve, riser, fastball, change—something she was doing was tipping off her rise ball. The first three batters seemed to be waiting for it, though they each made outs.

During the second inning, two batters in a row laid back on the risers, as if they knew what pitch was coming. They let it get in a little closer than usual—since it starts out looking just like a fastball—and they either let it go by for a ball or ripped it if it was a strike. One hit a single into center field, and the other sailed a line drive into the gap in left-center.

With one run in and no outs, and a runner on second, it was not a great start to the inning. Glory stood inside the pitcher's circle and stared at me—yeah, right, like it was my fault.

All I could do was shrug and keep playing. Kayla, who was catching, called time and ran out to talk to Glory. The other infielders joined them. Out of that meeting came the idea of using more fastballs, instead of risers, to set up her drop-curves and changeups, and that's what she did.

It really turned out to be a killer pitch combo. She'd

throw the first pitch up there on the outside corner at about sixty-five miles per hour. Then she'd follow with an off-speed pitch on the inside corner at about fifty. No one could guess—or time—the pitches, and the RaveRiders went on to win, 4–2.

This was a double-elimination tournament, which meant, as Madeline explained it to me, a team was eliminated after its second loss. By the end of game two, only six teams remained. Four were in the losers' bracket, with one loss apiece. And two teams, the RaveRiders and a fired-up black-and-gold pep squad from Costa Mesa, remained undefeated.

"I know what I was doing wrong," Glory told me after the game. "Kayla thought they were stealing her signs, but on my rise balls, I was starting off with my hip more to the right, so I could put a little more power on the ball as it left my hand. Someone noticed that, and that's how they knew when that pitch was coming. They were just waiting for it."

"It's all rocket science to me," I told her. And I was not exaggerating. Fast-pitch softball was the quickest sport I'd ever seen. Everything happened at high speed, and there was a lot to follow. "I'm glad you guys figured it out."

"Wasn't me, it was Kayla and Dakota." She dumped the rest of her water bottle onto her head, then gave her hair a shake. "Feels like it's ninety-five degrees out there."

"When's your next game?"

"Three-thirty. We have about an hour. But I won't be pitching. I get to rest." She smiled.

Sweet, I thought, that means I'll get to practice. "Who do you play?"

"Some big Amazon team from Orange County. They're undefeated, too. If we lose, we have to play one more game today against another team in the losers' bracket."

"Four games in one day?"

"It's happened before."

I shook my head. "And if you win?"

"We get to go home, crash, and burn."

"You better win."

"Right now, I just need to get out of the sun for a while and ice down my arm." She glared at me, adding, "Which is fine, by the way."

I held my hands up. "Did I say anything?"

"No, but I know how you think."

She began walking toward the shade of a blue-tarp awning, and I followed, saying, "Call me when the game's over. I'll be at Tran's. Dakota knows the number."

"Fine."

By five-thirty that afternoon, Maggie the Fireball had sent the Amazons to the losers' bracket as well, forcing them to be the ones to play one more game today. And the RaveRiders were free to gloat.

"So meet us at Hodad's," Glory yelled into the phone over the celebration behind her. I hated to call off band practice, but the other guys jumped all over the chance, so we did.

By the time the whole team and I had stampeded Hodad's and stuffed ourselves on floats, malts, fries, and burgers, there were only two teams still alive for tomorrow's grand finale. The future Olympians from Ocean Beach and a team of tired Amazon warriors from Orange County.

independence is overrated

Glory and I left Hodad's early so she could get a good night's sleep, but we walked slowly to her place, so we could also have a good talk.

"I just realized," said Glory, "tomorrow is going to be the biggest day of our lives."

"I know." I'd been feeling that in my gut all night long, actually. "And it's also Independence Day." I watched her face to see if she'd react.

It took a moment. "That'd be nice. I could use some independence."

A breeze caught several strands of her hair that had escaped her ponytail. But I didn't think of the music in that tickle of motion. I thought about being alone and how I always felt worse—how a big black cloud loomed up and darkened my mood—when I was by myself. How I seemed to be constantly worried about some dreadful event, though I had no idea what it could be. And how those feelings were now showing up even when I was with Glory.

"You know what I think?" I asked. "I think independence is overrated, if it means you're going to be lonely."

"Who's lonely?"

We turned left, up Bacon, and I wondered if I should tell her the truth, how bummed I'd been feeling lately, despite all the good news, how I was starting to believe I was cheating my way into the spotlight, despite what Dad had told me about Max Lucero.

"Nobody," I said. "Just an observation. So, look. When's your game tomorrow?"

"Starts at noon. And you guys play at three, right?"

"Two-thirty."

"Okay. And you're gonna be on that balcony above the Dharma Meditation Center?"

"Right. Overlooking Newport, on the corner nearest the beach. But you'll have to come around to the back stairs, next to the alley by the parking lot."

"Okay, that's cool. Here's what'll happen." She put one hand on my chest. "We'll beat those guys really quick, be out of there by one-thirty or two, and the tournament will be all over and done with. Then the Ravers will storm Newport with me. I will cause you to play like a man possessed—because I do inspire you, this I know—so you'll be sure to ace your auditions, and then you and I can hang out for the rest of the day, just by ourselves."

"And the night. We have to see the fireworks show on the pier, remember?"

"Oh, yeah, definitely."

I hated to bring up another scenario, but I needed to. "What if you guys lose?"

She jutted out a lip. "No problem. There'd be a final playoff game, but it wouldn't start till four, so I could still be there for your concert, then cruise on back to Robb Field in time for the game."

That was a big relief. Even after how well I'd been playing lately, how we'd totally killed at the street fair, this gig was for all the marbles. I didn't want to take any chances. I needed her for this one. After that—we'd see. "So are you pitching the first game tomorrow?"

"Yeah. That's why Maggie threw the last one today."

"Cool."

"That is, I'm supposed to."

"What's that mean?"

"Means it depends on how honest I am."

Now I knew. Things you fear may be closer than they appear. I reached my arm around behind her and cupped my hand on her right shoulder. I didn't say—or want to say—anything. Just gave her a gentle squeeze.

As we turned up Voltaire, she began sniffling. "What's wrong with me?" She stared straight ahead, into the hills above town. "I'm fine one day, I'm in pain the next. Then the next day, I'm fine again. Today, I was both! I *hate* this."

I had no clue. But it did seem as if, somehow, my

music had messed her up, her windup, her delivery, her release—something. I mean, for all I knew, maybe when I was helping her the most, she was actually in the most pain, but she couldn't feel it. Like I was putting a spell on her.

As we approached OB Juan's, Glory pulled me down to a bus bench, saying, "I don't want to go home yet."

"Okay." The night was cool, but not cold. The stars were visible and so was the moon. Most of it.

Looking where I was looking, she said, "Tomorrow's the baseball moon, Andy. That means it's been twenty-eight days since all this started."

I snapped my fingers. "And it went by like that."

"Liar."

"Am not. You know how time flies when you're—"

"Playing weird music in the alley so a loony girl can play her best at tryouts? Climbing up a backstop to save a crazy girl?"

"No. That—okay, that? That backstop thing was a new workout routine for trumpet players. You know, strengthens the hands, the grip. We should really do it on a regular basis. Like, once a year."

"Oh, right!" She pushed a flat hand against my shoulder. "See? It's been strange, at the least, you'd have to say. First, your music does this trippy thing to me. Then I make you come to all my softball stuff and keep doing it for me. Then you get all virtuoso when you do. And now we're these crazy, codependent enablers stuck with each other for all infinity." She nestled a shoulder into me. "Or something."

"That's cool." Codependent? I thought. For infinity? That's a fairly long time.

"Dracemon! And Marlina's little girl!"

We both turned to our left to see HoJo, the barefoot holy man, cruising up toward us. "Why do you always call me that?" Glory asked.

The Holy Jokester spoke through a toothy smile. "I love your mama, baby dah. She is one so fine."

"Well, in that case, you may call me any name you wish."

"Okay. Your name is now a dish delish. Tangerine Ice Cream."

"Hey, I like it," she said.

HoJo walked around in front of us, standing on the red curb. "Now tell to me, Tangerine Ice Cream, where are you going? What is your dream?"

"I'm going where I'm always going when I see you, Holy Mon. I'm going to ask you a questy-on."

"Then, good-bye, we'll speak when you get back."

She waved both hands. "I'm there and back already."

"Ya, ya, rock steady. So what's the quest, one who's blessed?"

"Am I? See, that's really what I wanted to know.

This thing between Andy and me, what do you think so far?"

" 'Tis a fusion of delusion, of optical intrusions. Here today, gone to sorrow. Tell me, Drace, what do you embrace?"

I nodded slowly. "I think you're hammer on, mon. I got no bif.'

"Ah, well, the radar's down all over the 'hood. I'm jamma-jamma wit O-lee-via, and it's all no good. Now she da jokester and I'm da terrible tarot bull, mon." He leaned in toward Glory. "What can I do, Marlina's Tangerina, tell me true."

"Just keep trying, HoJo. We know you're doing your best."

"Thank you, pretty girl. I will try till de enda da whirl."

He spun around and slapped our palms, both ways, and I echoed Glory's appreciation. Who knows what he could come up with? I thought. Anything would help.

Pushing his hands toward the sidewalk like he was dribbling two basketballs at once, he said, "We never had this con, mon." Then he left faster than he'd arrived, like he couldn't wait to get out of here. Over his shoulder, he called, "Catch you on the flip trip."

"Adiós" I called back. "Good luck."

Glory grabbed my arm, pulling me closer. "What do

you think about that? HoJo seemed nervous, and I've never seen him nervous before."

I agreed. He did seem edgier than usual. But that was a judgment call when it came to the Jokester. "I don't know. He didn't even tell us we were free to go."

"There's something strange happening here."

"In OB? How can you tell?"

"I don't know. It's just a weird feeling I have." Glory let out a breath and snuggled next to me a while longer, then put both arms around me, clasping her fingers together on my shoulder. For a while, we just sort of sat there and looked at the street and the cars passing by.

"Andy?"

"Hmm."

"What's it going to be like? In the future? You know, when you're a big music star and everything and I'm a professional softball player. Tell me what you see, when both of us are living our dreams."

"Well, okay." I tried to picture it. "We're going to be totally happy, first off. Rich, famous, and happy. We'll have the fastest, coolest cars, so we can zip around everywhere we go, like to jazz festivals and World Cup softball games and—and movie premieres."

"Movie premieres?"

"Yeah. When they make the story of my life."

"*Your* life?"

"I mean, *our*, um, *love* story and . . . and . . ."

"Do we have any children?"

"You kidding? We start off with five. You know, so they can be a jazz quintet. Then we add four more so they can be the coolest, jazziest traveling softball team in the world."

She tightened around me. I had no idea where all that had come from. I think I just sensed it was what Glory needed to hear. Or what I wanted to hear. It had to be happy, I knew that. After all, Dad said being happy was most important. And even Mad Max said all he wanted for me was happiness. And I was sure it was coming. It had to be. Maybe after tomorrow.

"I like that," she said, in a low voice.

Me, too. We just needed to get through tomorrow, I decided. If we could manage to do that, so many good things would follow that none of this little stuff would matter. My irritations, Glory's weird pain. All that would just sort of disappear, is what I figured. FuChar Skool and I have a shot at stardom. We just need to get through tomorrow, that's all. And of course, we have to blow some minds.

I dug feeling her warm breath on my neck as I looked up at the sky. I found the Big Dipper and when I really looked, I thought I saw faint traces of the trumpet stars. How they'd burned so bright that one night, I'd probably never know. Or maybe I'd never want to know.

Glory's eyes were closed, and I could hear her rubbing the seashells on her necklace between her thumb and fingers. I loved that sound.

"Why do you and your mom always wear those seashell necklaces?"

"Mom says they represent our Indian heritage. My grandparents are part Shoshone, and those Indians used to live up the coast, near Oceanside." She tangled her fingers into the shells, rattling them. "But to me, they make me feel connected to Mom. I mean, even when we fight, and I hate her and everything? I hold these and I always know we're connected. We have each other."

"That's cool. My dad's part Indian, too. I think almost all Mexicans are. My mom's mostly Irish, though, so I'm basically a mixed-up kid."

Her response was to tighten her arms around me.

And my mind traveled again into tomorrow, where mile-high-profile gigs were just waiting for us. A West Coast road tour, recording time at the coolest studios, using the highest tech equipment around, a record deal. And that's just in the first few months, it sounded like. Max said he could do things in an instant—and after this week, I didn't doubt him on that. I realized the way Max was causing certain breaks to open up for me, by taking the opportunities from other bands, was not the coolest, but I figured once I was set up in the biz, then those other bands could pick up right where they left off. No harm. It wasn't like I'd have to walk on them forever.

But me, I had to ride this wild horse while I could. Why should I set it aside and go on trying to get a foothold? I knew what happened then. When you needed it back, you'd get stuck right where you were. Because by then, that wild horse was gone.

ah, the nonchalance of truth

During the first game Sunday morning, disaster struck.

Coach Becca did not start Glory. She apparently noticed Glory still seemed to be in pain. How honest Glory was about it in their private conversation, I didn't know, but Becca decided to start Maggie and hold Glory in reserve. Thing was, Maggie did not have today what she had yesterday against this same team.

Four runs in the first inning and three runs in the second put the game out of reach, though I noticed no one ever said so. In the third, Becca brought in Lizzie, who's a lefty and a lot of fun to be around, but she was mainly there to stop the bleeding and try to avoid the ten-run mercy rule. She didn't. By the time I decided to leave, the score was 11–0, and if the RaveRiders didn't score that inning—the 6th—the game was over.

"Glory," I said through the dugout screen, "I'm going to the street party. I'll see you there, okay?"

She had her foot up on the bench, sitting sideways. "Yeah, okay, what time is it?"

I reached into my pocket for my one-dollar digital. "It's 1:59. We're starting in half an hour."

Glory held her hand up near my face, twisting it sideways, zipping it around, while she made tiny motor noises.

I laughed, and so did she. Already we'd gone beyond words on the "I'll Be There" deal. That would save me a whole lot of thinking at times like these.

"Just remember," she reminded me, "the real, true, final championship game starts at four. Okay? Because no matter what, I'm going to pitch. And I'm really gonna need you." As soon as she said that, she started smiling, knowing she'd set me up for my own little spaceship ride.

I made much better noises. Jet engines, squealing tires burning rubber, and I even flew my hand into my hat, so it looked like a little headless doll bopping through the air.

"Okay, okay," she said, waving me off. "You are so free to get out of here that I don't even want to see you again until I'm on that balcony, all right?" She immediately squeezed her eyes shut, then clamped her hands over her ears, realizing that once again she'd set me up, and my "IBT" rocket was ready to roar.

Finally, I split and rolled down Abbott Street, along the beach, thinking how I dug the way Glory could mindshake me out of being so over-the-top serious about my music. The Fourth of July crowd started getting really thick just before I reached Newport, where I skated into a total surfer-fratboy-hippie-Rasta-Raza-

Indo-Euro-multi-eth street jam, with tatt skin, tanned skin, and big grins flashing everywhere. Cool, totally mellow vibes, all good people. It was going to be a blast rocking this road to the rooftops.

I picked up my board and maneuvered my way to the stairwell located at the back of the building, trying to spot any blinged-up, L.A.-looking Gucci dudes who might be here to scope out me and the band.

"Oh, and where have you been?" Walking toward me from the foot of the stairs was Max Lucero, with a wily smile a mile wide. "Ah, the nonchalance of youth. You have twelve minutes till showtime."

"That's cool," I said, noticing that my throat had tightened and that I was feeling twinges of fear pulsing through me, just looking at his jack-o'-lantern grin. "What are you so happy about?" I asked.

He walked with me to the wooden stairway.

"I live for moments like these, Andrés. But please, my friend. One word of caution. In this crowd there are record producers, executives, club owners, and booking agents."

I listened intently, with my heart rate rising, as he continued.

"I have worked long and hard to disarrange the fates of many to bring you this golden horse of an opportunity."

Whoa. Now I began to sweat. Felt like icewater was covering my skin. Was I really hearing this? The guy was no joke, for sure. He definitely had powers I did not understand.

"I understand," I said.

"Good." Then he lowered his voice. "You will thrill. They will marvel. And deals will be struck." He was almost giddy as he spoke. "Provided we have no distractions."

"Distractions?"

"The girl," he said with a soft smile. "She no longer matters to us. Perhaps you have noticed. She has become a distraction."

"What are you talking about? Glory?"

I could hear Tran and Lil Lobo tuning up and getting set. They didn't even know I'd arrived. It was time for me to go.

"Max, look. What I do up onstage, that's just between us, you and me. I don't know—I don't even want to know—how you made this happen. And, man, I really, really appreciate the whole opportunity you've given me. But Glory's not in on this. And she's no distraction."

"Once upon a time," said Max, "when we needed the publicity, she was useful. She was good for a headline or two, something to turn the spotlight your way. But in truth, she is no more than a typical above-average softball pitcher. The world is full of them. And more to the point, she will not be pitching again."

I shook with a panic I had never felt before, as if a

jug of acid had been pumped directly into my stomach. My legs weakened. I suddenly and thoroughly realized my little handshake with Max had earthquaked through the lives of many innocent people. The words marched slowly, fearfully, out of my mouth. "You hurt Glory? On purpose?"

"Ah," he said calmly, "let us say, the clock has struck midnight on her, and now she must leave the ball behind." He stopped to admire his twisted humor with a twisted grin. "For her to linger on would make her a mindshaking distraction."

"No, you're wrong. You're dead wrong." I had too much to process, and this was not the time to do it. "I gotta go. I'm late. But this ain't over, pal."

I started up the stairs on woozy legs. He stuck his cane across my path.

"Look, Max, you're killing me here. Stop it! Ever since I said okay to you, I haven't been myself, I've been so worried about all this stuff. And now I—" Tears were brimming. I couldn't believe it. No, man, I told myself. Don't stand here and start crying.

"Andrés." Max's face was filled with light. His little eyes were dancing. "No need to be emotional. My goodness, no." He breathed in a sorry-sounding laugh.

I could hear Tran begin his stretched-string, feedback-heavy Jimi Hendrix version of "The Star-Spangled Banner." The show had started without me.

But Tran knew, if he had to, he could run that song out for six or eight minutes, and no one in OB would mind.

Max lowered his cane. "I simply wish to remind you of our agreement. And of how much we depend upon each other for what we desire."

Now the anger burned through me. "Then why are you doing this? My brain's spinning from the time I wake up. I'm in a bad mood all day long. I—I don't want you helping me anymore, okay? I don't want you hurting Glory and disarranging—disarranging anyone's life anymore!"

"But this is what you wished for, my boy."

"I did not. You said I'd be happy. And I believed you. But I'm not. As far as I'm concerned, you lied. The deal's off."

"I misrepresented nothing. Not one thing. I was quite clear."

"Look. You said all you wanted was to see me happy. And, yeah, when the contracts come in, and the money starts flying, maybe I will be. But I'm not now, and you're making me feel worse."

Max smiled calmly. "Ah, but I'm afraid you misrepresent me. What I said was, 'All I want is your happiness.'"

"Right."

His smile grew larger. "And now I have it. I believe it was a fair trade."

My blood chilled. My heart stopped beating, and my hands turned cold. I could not breathe. *Oh. Oh, no.*

He put his hand on my shoulder. "You can do what you want, my friend. If you are not pleased, walk away. Or you can take advantage of this great future and forget your past. So dry your tears, I say. But I have lived up to my part of the bargain. And I'm afraid you shall have to do so as well."

He tipped his hat, turned, and started walking away. I thought about grabbing him and throwing him against a wall. Pulverizing the little lizard. But at that point, I could barely stand. I felt sick from my gut to my throbbing head. Besides, he had all the power. And it was a thousand times more than I'd ever had.

I was trapped. He knew it. And he knew that I knew it.

desperado

I froze where I stood, paralyzed, as scene after scene from the past two weeks movie-screened through my mind. Glory in pain, me brain-spun, whipped into song-writing frenzies, losing sleep, feeling angry and depressed.

How could I have been so blind, so dumb, so unable to hear what the man had said to me over and over again? All he wanted was my happiness, and I gave it to him. And of course that's what he wanted. I mean, the dude didn't even know how to laugh. His idea of humor was to get a street gang of snails to tag my sidewalk.

At least I didn't throw up and I didn't cry. I took in a huge breath, balanced myself, and hustled up the stairs. Tran looked up, saw me rushing to the balcony corner, and grinned. That helped. He brought it on down. Lil Lobo sizzled the cymbals, leading into a final drumroll. Immediately I was in there with them both, inside the anthem, as the song reminded me of the town I lived in. OB actually was the land of the free and the home of the brave. And now I was determined to prove it. I was ready to lead the fusion charge where no one had ever gone before.

Only thing missing was Glory.

As I made my way alongside Tran, I kept scanning the edges of the crowd and thinking that it could not be taking her this long. But I also knew it was out of my control. All I could do now was play.

We started off with a couple of our new songs, and the improv stuff went great, but, man, it was not the same without Glory. The fun was gone; the soul was gone. It seemed so hollow, so empty. But maybe that was just the Max effect lingering on. Maybe things would improve. Five minutes, ten minutes rolled by.

During the next song, I leaned my hip against the balcony rail, playing with my eyes closed, like some New Orleans brass cat, thinking I might be able to dream her up, when someone gently touched my arm. I opened my eyes.

Marlina Martinez stood at my side. "Andy, Glory sent me."

I quit the solo, and Lil Lobo brought it on down into a wicked roar of applause, whoops, and whistles. But without that certain maverick mischief I felt around Glory that drove my improvs, that filled my soul, I could only flash the crowd a phony, goony, scarecrow grin.

"Where is she? I *need* her." What I really needed

was to see her. To know she was no longer in pain. My pain. I remembered the way I had left her.

"It's a big mess," said Mrs. Martinez. "The tournament director decided to move up the final game time rather than risk losing the crowd to the street celebration and not having them come back. So Glory is playing her championship game *now*."

"She's pitching?"

"She was trying to."

Lil Lobo stared at me from behind his drums. "Dude," he said, fully emphasizing the importance of this development.

Tran held his guitar neck up near his ear, ready to race into the next song. They both needed me to count out the beat on this one—our bust-out-of-the-country tune I had written especially for today, "When They Outlaw Freedom." It was also our first real chance to show the crowd our finest set of chops.

I turned and saw Max had reappeared. He was now up on the balcony with us, standing at the far south end, just grinning. I rushed him, pushing a few rock fans out of my way, and got right in his craggy, smirky, happy little face.

"You did this! You made her schedule change so it would clash with mine."

"You left me little choice. Look at yourself. Now even her absence distracts you. Nothing else is keeping you from showing your passion, from showing these powerful producers what you can do. Nothing, Andrés, but her hold on you."

He had me in his claws and he was squeezing. Record producers. Club owners. Even Glory would want me to shine for them. If she really was pitching right now, what could I do about it anyway?

"This is the moment, my boy, that will decide your destiny. Go back to your band and play for us and enjoy the riches of your labor. If not, you will lose it all. You will never come this close to fame and fortune again."

I turned and slowly walked back. I couldn't think of anything else to do. But I hated to give in—to give up—to him.

I looked at Glory's mom. Could she? I wondered. Could she sub for Glory, for just one song, to bring back some fun? Maybe grab a tambourine, stand next to me, and sway? I thought it was worth a try. Just for one song, to show this crowd, the promoters, the A&R guys, and whoever else was out there, what a desperado like me could really do under the influence of love.

I looked at my dad, standing near our equipment on the street side of the stage. His face was full of concern. Now that he was finally behind me one hundred percent, he didn't understand the half of it. And he certainly couldn't comprehend this silence. I glanced back at Mrs. Martinez. And then my mind zoomed. It flew off to a place full of passion and pure of heart. I may never know why, but something drew my eyes up Newport Avenue, over Dad's shoulder, up over the hill and into the eastern sky. There I saw, big as day, the baseball moon. And I knew what I had to do. My future depended upon it. I put my arm around Glory's mom, and said, "Will you please sing 'Desperado'?"

She grabbed my wrist. "Oh, no, honey. I can't."

"Please? It would really mean a lot."

"Andy, you know I haven't been onstage in years."

"Well." I took a step back and shrugged. "Neither have I." I gave her a crooked grin. "Besides, Glory says you're the Karaoke Queen of Arizona. And, look. Just one song. We're losing the crowd here."

My dad stepped in between us with a guitar in his hand. He'd heard the whole thing. "I'll play the acoustic behind you, Marlina. Let's try it. Like old times. It'll be all right."

My poor dad. He was now the recipient of the infamous Martinez-girl staredown. But it didn't shake him one bit. Right in front of Mom and the whole town, he put his thick tattooed arm around her and kissed the side of her face. "It's your song, Lina. Bless us with it? Hmm?"

She did not answer out loud. Widening her eyes and blinking rapidly, she just shook her head, looking straight at my dad. Then she glanced at Tran, took a giant breath, and said, "In the key of D, boys."

I handed her the mic from the stand. I shot a sharp look at Lil Lobo and Tran, lifting my chin at them both. "This is it, *carnalitos*. I'm counting on you guys to tear it up. Okay? I mean, tear it up, for me and for Glory. You have to blow down some walls."

"Dude?" said Lil Lobo, asking me with his eyes what was going on.

I tapped my heart. It was on fire. Then I motioned toward the stairway with my thumb. He understood.

Turning to Dad, I said, "I gotta go, Pop. Help these guys out, will you?"

I didn't let him respond. Grabbing my skateboard and horn, I ran past everyone—even ol' Max—across the balcony, down the back stairs, and through the crowd.

"You will regret this," called Max.

I bet I will, I thought. But not as much as I regret this whole deal.

Last thing I heard as I disappeared into the heart of OB was Mrs. Martinez's very first line, delivered slow and fine, in an a cappella quiver. It was easy to hear, once the hush took hold. I heard my dad fall in behind her with his crisp acoustic, playing firm, but easy. And I carried away with me a velvet-voiced angel asking, for all to hear, why don't I come to my senses?

Of course, as I gunned it down the middle of Abbott, skating as fast as I could fly, I truly believed that for the first time this summer, I had done just that.

from here to infinity and back again

I reached Glory's ball game in the top of the second inning. I'd heard the huge softball crowd yelling from two blocks away, but hustling through the park and seeing all the families, friends, and fans stomping, cheering, and clapping really showed me how much this game meant to a lot of people.

The RaveRiders were in the field. I saw that Costa Mesa had a runner on every base, but the pitcher was not Glory. I looked for her in the dugout and in the bleachers, but she wasn't there either.

I ran up to home plate. "Kayla!" I called through the screen. "What's going on? Where's Glory?"

Kayla spun around and looked surprised to see me. "Time, Blue," she called, and ran back to me. "What are you doing here, Andy?"

"What do you mean? Where's Glory?"

"She left. Don't you guys have a concert? She went to be with you."

My heart spun a 360 and slid down a half-pipe. I didn't say another word, but pushed myself off the chain-link screening and sprinted back across the grass.

We must've taken parallel streets, I figured, and passed each other along the way. I could not have imagined a nightmare scenario worse than this. Now we both were missing our showcase events, our dream moments. And it wasn't because they didn't happen. They were simply happening without us.

What if she gets there, I wondered, sees I'm gone, then turns around and runs back? And I miss her again? This could go on forever!

Approaching the street, I was nearly dead. My legs felt like they were running against ocean breakwater like in one of Glory's drills. Finally on asphalt, I could ride and I launched my board across West Point Loma Boulevard. A few blocks later, as I raced up to Long Branch, I saw a crazy dream-chaser, in full softball uniform, charging at me from the north.

I swung left, pushing harder, and lifted my horn. Rolling along, I played the ocean wavetop bop of her head, rising above the parked cars with each long-legged stride, falling with each footplant onto the concrete. I couldn't help it.

That was all she needed to hear. She slowed to an easier pace, cruising right up to me, and burst into tears.

She fell against my chest, exhausted, crying hard, then started tugging my arm. "Come on," she said. "You have to get back."

"Wait, wait, wait," I said. "I'm not going back."

"Andy, you're crazy. We have to go."

"No, we don't. We're going to your game. It's more important. It really is."

"No, it's not. It's too late. I didn't even pitch." She dragged the back of her hand over each eye.

"Doesn't matter. They need you now, and to me, your game's more important."

"I don't believe you. Why are you saying that?"

"I have to explain later." I took her arm the way Kayla had taken mine along this street a lifetime ago. "Come on. Please!"

"Are you sure?" I heard the slightest note of relief in her voice.

"Yes," I said, and finally Glory did not resist.

Except to draw in a breath and gasp out three little words. "I'm there already."

around the horn

By the time we arrived back at Robb Field, ballpark Number Two, I could barely stand. The game was in the top of the fourth inning and the score was tied, 3–3.

Waiting for Kayla and the others to get their third out and come in to hit, Glory stood on the sidelines pitching softly to one of her teammates, going through her motions.

I hung out a few feet from her, not playing, just talking. "Let's pick up where we left off yesterday," I said.

She hummed agreement, collecting herself, focusing on the field.

Seeing Glory ready to pitch seemed to help her whole team. They knew her and they knew what her day had been like. It was a miracle to see her here. Returning to the dugout at the bottom of the fourth, their enthusiasm spilled out.

"Let's bust it open, ladies," Dakota called, clapping her hands. "Let's get a bunch."

Kayla shouted, "Who's up? Who's up? Glory, are you in the game?"

"I don't know." She looked at Becca, who I believed must've known more about teenage girls than anyone on the planet to still be so calm after all of this.

"Not yet," she said. "You're coming in to pitch the top of the fifth and then you'll take over for Maggie in the batting order."

The top of the fifth was coming right up, because at the moment, if there was any girl showing any rhythm, any music, any dance in that game, it was the pitcher from Costa Mesa. She had just struck out three batters in a row, and the RaveRiders took the field.

As Glory approached the mound, I set up along the fence just past third base. I played quiet little spurts, popping my lips, nothing serious. On Glory's last warm-up toss, I blew a little harder. But as I watched her respond, something did not seem right. Her arm looked fine—it had a lot of snap—but her legs had no spring in them at all.

If she could just get through this inning, I figured, then she could rest and let her legs recover. But, as I soon saw, that was not going to happen. Her mechanics were too out of sync, and nothing I did seemed to work; it only seemed to make matters worse. The first two hitters walked, then she pegged the next one in the ribs. A single up the middle brought in two more runs, and that brought out her coach, who called for another pitcher. Quick as that. Glory switched places with the girl in center field—Lizzy, the team's third pitcher—

whose job now was to keep the situation from getting any worse. At 5–3, the game could still be won.

I looked at my watch. Twenty minutes of concert time left. Glancing off toward the center of town, I imagined my route. By my calculation, I could still show up for the last fifteen minutes. After what I'd gone through today, I also imagined tearing the place up with those guys, just ripping it open and seeing how long I could keep on going. Really, I was at the point where I had no fear left in me at all. I mean, I finally felt like the Fool.

I glanced toward Glory. She was looking anywhere but back at me. I knew there was no good reason for me to remain at the ballpark, but I wanted to wave good-bye at least. I began to back away, watching her.

After the next pitch, I took one more step back and played a couple of notes. Glory was lost in her world, palms on her knees, eyes cast downward. But I did notice Kayla turn her head my way.

Through her catcher's mask I could not see her eyes or her expression. Probably she was just checking, curious to see what I was doing. And you know what? My feet would not move another step. Don't ask me why, but at that moment, I felt rooted to this ball field, this spot, this situation.

Realizing I had just made a huge decision—and feeling fearless about it—I walked back in, toward the fence, and rested my elbows on the top pipe. Going back, I knew, would've been my only chance at redemption. And a shot at the big time.

So I went through Grandpa's checklist. Where was my passion? Well, at the moment, my passion was in center field. I was here for her. Did I have a pure heart and a purpose generous in spirit? Yes, the same as I had the moment I decided to leave the concert. So, *Abuelito*, I guess my decision stands.

He didn't need to answer. I felt it.

Besides, I told myself, she might pitch again. And then she'd need me to be there. To be behind her a hundred percent.

Nothing had changed by the top of the seventh and final inning. Lizzy was doing really well, but the score was still 5–3.

When the RaveRiders came in for their last at-bats, I watched Glory run straight toward me, removing her mouthpiece, and tucking it under the shoulder strap inside her jersey. "You don't have to stay anymore," she said, grabbing the top of the fence. "This is hopeless."

"No problem. My gig's over, anyway." I had already resolved myself to the situation and its aftermath. You see, not a single new song or tune had rolled through my brain since I'd arrived here—so when I said it was over, I meant more than she could know. "But, hey, did I mention that your mom was singing for us when I left?"

"No! Really?"

"She totally saved the show." I was actually sounding upbeat about it. "My dad was playing acoustic behind her, and it was sounding really cool."

Glory rolled her eyes. "I'm so sorry. I wish you could've stayed. I wish we could've followed our plan."

"No worries," I said with a small smile. "I'm sorry you guys won't be Firecracker champions." I turned to the crowd. "Any scouts show up?"

"How would I know? I hope not. I stunk up the joint."

"You didn't. You were off today. Or, to be honest, I was."

"I'll be lucky if I'm not off the team." She stepped away from the fence and began wandering toward her dugout, saying, "I don't know why Becca would want me after today."

Having no answer for her, I strolled back through the many clusters of fans sitting on the grass. Back toward the handball courts. I figured I'd sit down a while and wait until the final out. When I got there and looked back at the field, I realized that so much had changed since I was here last.

Four weeks ago, I held all this hope for my "breakout summer." Over that time, though, I'd been given two great chances to advance my career, to help me break out. Two swings, you might say, at two perfect pitches, and two totally embarrassing misses. Ah, well,

I decided. As a musician, I knew that "perfect pitch" was overrated. That having *heart* counts for a lot more.

But I also knew that whatever special effect my music once had on Glory was gone as well. And that felt like strike three.

This will now be known, I decided, as my "strike-out" summer.

Sitting there on the concrete, running the events of the month through my mind, took me once again to a sad place, and I supposed I'd better get used to it.

But it took only one huge cheer—an explosion from the stands—to bring me right back into this world. And the game.

I stood up to see two runners digging around the bases and finally coming to a halt at second and third. Whoa! I rushed back toward the field and realized the bases were loaded with RaveRiders.

Then I saw Kayla walking up to the plate, wiggling her shoulders, swinging the bat around like a weight bar. She stepped into the batter's box and stood staring at the pitcher with professional cool.

She twisted her back foot, working her shoe into the dirt, as if sinking it into wet sand.

I hummed something in my head, tempted to shoot a few notes her way.

But before I did anything, the pitcher delivered, and Kayla ripped it right back at her—past her!—and into center field.

I either jumped by my own excitement or was lifted up by the tremendous roar that rose from a crowd gone berserk. In one blue-eyed swing, the game was tied!

The screaming, the stomping, the noisemaking lasted for nearly a full minute as the other pitcher bent over, walked around the mound, and generally fumed while her coach tried to talk to her.

Madeline, the winning run, was standing on third base, kicking her toes into the bag. And from way over at first, Kayla was looking right at me and making small circles in the air with her hand.

I held my palms in the air. "What?"

She swung her arms and pointed toward home plate. I leaned over the fence. Glory was standing next to Becca, taking practice swings.

Oh, wow. No DH today? She's actually going to bat?

I started tapping the horn, bobbing my head, wetting my lips. She took two more full cuts. And I saw it all. Every motion, every little thing she did, all those little pieces of her swing from those magical, mysterious moments four weeks ago—before I even knew who she was—came flooding back.

So I painted her—playing as if my fingers were separate from my brain.

Rest, ready, step, swing.

Wha-uuu. Ta-da-dee. Ta. Ta-boom.

Any little hit at all would score the winning run from third.

Rest, ready, step, swing.

Wha-uuu. Ta-da-dee. Ta. Ta-boom.

She didn't need to swing like crazy. Or throw off her mechanics. Or throw off her rhythm with some battle-whack of a swing.

Any little hit was going to be just fine.

It did not have to be the booming, high-tower home run she slammed through the trees beyond the center-field fence on the very next pitch.

But it was.

And in the moments that followed Glory's blast, no one, including me, could hear my trumpet, since the screaming, crying, whistling, and cheering were so loud. I just remember blaring away as I saw Glory begin her graceful dance around the bases, around the horn, after watching the ball she had just crushed disappear into this mad, beautiful afternoon, under the baseball moon.

you gotta fight for your right to be gnarly

OB Juan threw the RaveRiders a party no one will ever forget. He invited the whole town. Everything was half price. Holistic chair massages and tarot card readings were being donated free of charge. Dakota's mom brought along two masseuses from ShapeShifters, and Olivia was back to her normal self again, a fact she wanted everyone to know.

The famous OB Fireworks Show, scheduled to blast off at nine from the pier that night, was a huge tradition. But as eight-thirty rolled around, no one seemed to be leaving. Didn't matter either way to me. I was so tired, I could've gone to sleep on a tabletop, except that all the girls dancing on them would've woken me up.

"Why so glum?" asked Glory, walking back from the buffet table with two plates of tacos, rice, and beans.

"Sorry. I'm just tired." For the first time in days, I had a genuine reason to feel bummed, not just because I was cursed.

"Here, I brought you something to eat."

I smiled. "Thanks. Comfort food."

"Verdad.' She took a delicate bite.

"Kayla and Maggie parked their plates here, a while ago," I said, waving at their food, "but I haven't seen them since." Far more people were roaming around the place, dancing in conga lines, and chasing down friends, than were sitting and eating.

OB Juar came on the sound system to make a request for all RaveRiders to meet him at the stage.

Glory set down her taco. "Save this for me," she said, pushing her plate my way. I watched her weave through the crowd and join the other blue jerseys in front of the bandstand.

Coach Becca took the microphone and, going down the line, introduced all the players, mentioning something cool about each one.

"And our shortstop, Dakota," she said, near the end, "really started to contribute after she finally turned in a great play—for a boyfriend."

The whole team *whooed* and laughed. Dakota smiled calmly, her strong, dynamic throwing arm and hand intertwined with the narrow arm and fine fretting fingers of Tran's left hand.

"And, finally," Becca continued, "I want to present the heart and soul of our team, Glory Martinez." The ovation was huge. "We're used to seeing Glory win games for us on the mound, but today, she did it with her bat."

More whistles and cheers.

"Glor-ree, Glor-ree," her teammates began chanting. Soon the entire crowd was in on it. At last, Glory, obviously mortified, took the mic. She stood stiffly, not daring to look at anyone but her coach. "Thank you," she said. "Thanks to everyone, really. But all you guys know, I wouldn't be here tonight if it weren't for the amazing talent of the greatest trumpet player in the world, Andy Ramos."

Oh, curveball! No—a knockdown pitch.

People turned my way, pointing me out, waving. I was so not in the mood for any of this. Didn't matter to them, though. Before long, the place was rocking with the roar of "An-dee, An-dee, An-dee."

What did they want? I was nobody now, though they couldn't have known. I stood and waved like Dork the Jork, then sat back down. Didn't even faze them. "An-dee, An-dee."

Finally OB Juan grabbed the mic and said, "Come on up, Andrés. And bring your horn."

Oh, no. Anything but that. I thought about slipping my trumpet under the table and waving my empty hands. But I had it *on* the table. Besides, did I ever go anywhere without it?

Next, OB Juan called out to Tran and Lil Lobo to come onstage as well, telling us we could borrow the band equipment that was already set up for tonight's show.

"How about a couple of songs, guys?" asked OB Juan. Like we had any choice. I huddled with Tran.

"Let's do something heavy on guitar," I said. "I'll try to sing, but, man, my trumpet is outta commish."

He nodded. "How about 'That Night Down by the River'?"

"Cool." I stepped up to the mic stand and adjusted the height. "Thank you," I said. The crowd began to quiet down "We are—or at least we once were—FuChar Skool."

I gave Lil Lobo an upward chin nod. He raised his eyebrows and returned the nod. A moment later, he clicked off the beat. Tran jumped in, and they were off. Man, those guys could play. And the huge Marshall speakers stacked up behind us sent vibrations from my leg bones to my skull.

I started singing in a low bass voice. "Down, down, movin' on downtown, me and Bob Marley was a-rockin' away. I was down, down, groovin' at a stoplight, when I seen a woman lookin' my way. Yeah, I seen a woman lookin' my way."

At that moment my eyes found Glory's, and I did not sing the next few lines. Her face, her presence, her faith in me had suddenly brought me home. Back to my roots. Like the root doctor I'm sure she was, she had guided me to that place between two worlds, where only the fearless dare to go. My hand clenched the dented, poker-game trumpet next to my knee, and I played the only decent card I'd been dealt. I lifted the horn to my lips and, boys, I played the Fool.

That little golden Yamaha began articulating every syllable, every nuance, of that crazy song about the time I was skating to the sounds of a Marley CD and came upon Glory standing on the corner, next to Willie's Shoe Shine. At the crossroads.

I was not as good as I'd ever been. I was the *best* I had ever been. I had gone to the edge of my musical universe, ripped it open, and kept on going. We finished the song. We did one more. Then I invited my mom and dad to come up and join us for one last tune. Dude, I owned the place.

As soon as I made the request, Dad's eyes began blinking like a strobe. Sorry, Pop, I thought. I didn't plan on this either. Mom was conga dancing her way to the stage, her blond hair flying up and down, her whole face nothing but a grin.

I decided on something from their era, a truly stomp-on-the-floor and knock-down-the-door Tex-Mex version of that old Beastie Boys hit, "You Gotta Fight for Your Right (to Party!)."

Forget about it. I was surprised no one called the cops—or the earthquake center—especially when the street filled with dancers, even after the song was over.

Coming down off the stage, I really felt sorry for the band that had to follow us, but what could I do? I was so loopy, I didn't even know where to step, where to stand. All I could think to do was to rise up on my tiptoes and search for Glory. I spotted her and a few other Ravers against the side wall, still dancing away to the piped-in music. Instead of battling my way over to her, though, I decided to head outside, get some fresh air, and try to sift through what just happened.

What was different? What had changed? Why was I suddenly better than ever? Hey, maybe it was muscle memory. That was as good a guess as any.

I walked around the side of the building, keeping a low pro, brim down, no eye contact, and continued around to the back.

Pulling up next to the stairway to Glory's place, I leaned my back against it, folded my arms, and brought my hat over my face. My heart was still pumping hard against my forearms.

"Man," I whispered. "That was all right."

"All right?" said a voice behind me. I jumped and spun around, yanking off my hat. Hidden in the shadows beneath the stairwell stood Max Lucero. "It was sensational," he continued. "Ceremonial in nature. Full of passion, heart, and purpose."

"Hey," I said, staring into the dark, but not quite seeing him. "You don't have any power over me anymore."

"The only power I ever had was what you were willing to give up."

"You tricked me."

"Did I?"

I dropped my shoulders, relaxing a bit, regaining my honesty. "Well, maybe not entirely." What was the use of arguing the point, anyway? I knew what had gone wrong, and I wasn't completely blameless. "I guess I only heard what I wanted to hear."

"And so now you know."

"I know a lot more than I did before I met you, if that's what you mean."

Behind me in the distance, the fireworks started. I heard the initial rocket whistles, followed by the pops and booms.

"Your actions have shown that now you know what you need to know."

The entire area lit up. For a flash moment, I could see the man's face. But it wasn't Max. It was unlike any face I had seen.

In the successive bursts of brightness I put together the picture of the man I was talking to. Not some rumpled, elegant, Old World dude. He was just old. Weathered skin, a deep, deep tan. He stood tall. His long gray-and-black hair was parted into two braids that fell over the front of each shoulder. His only piece of clothing was a small patch of deerskin draped from his hips. He held a tall, hand-cut walking stick with several black feathers hanging down. This guy could've been centuries old. He could've walked out of these hills back in the Mission days with some of my own ancestors.

"Who are you?" I asked. "And you're saying, what? This was some kind of test or something?"

He stepped out of the darkness and into the light. "I am a friend of the family." The fireworks continued to burst all around in rapid order, lighting the man's face in greens and reds. "And this was no test. It was a school. For the future."

Around his neck I saw a string of white shells. Smooth, round, creamy white half shells. In the middle of the necklace hung a small, smoky-green horse carved from stone. A horse of jade. The next spray of light painted a blue starburst around his eye.

I could only stand there and stare.

"You know all you need to know," he said. "No more questions, Dracemon. Your grandfather sends his regards. You are free to go."

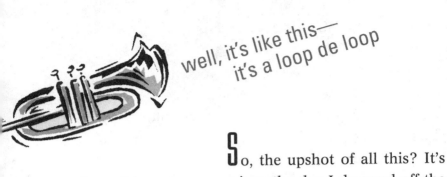

well, it's like this— it's a loop de loop

So, the upshot of all this? It's been three years now since the day I dropped off the music industry's radar screen and Glory lived up to her name in front of *three* college scouts who happened to be buried somewhere in that delirious Firecracker crowd.

And in those three years, Glory's mom has resurfaced as one of the top vocalists in California. The July Fourth gig launched her career, not mine. Some karma, eh? Some dharma.

And this spring, Glory picked through two full-ride offers and two partial athletic scholarships before deciding to move north with her jazzy mom and attend Cal Berkeley, all expenses paid. The Frisco jazz scene is the best in the West.

And me? I share a little two-bedroom apartment above OB Juan's with two disgusting roommates, three guitars, two drum sets, and at least one great song. It's a brassy, jazzed-up blend of reggae and rockabilly blues called "When They Outlaw Freedom, Only Outlaws Will Be Free."

Played it last Fourth of July—yeah, this time I

played—and we tore it up. Even the bikers in sleeveless black leather sitting at El Rodeo across the street barked recognition when the song ended, hooting even louder when Glory unfurled a banner off the rail reading "FuChɛr Skool is NOW in Session!"

Will we ever make it out of this town? Well, I won't answer that, since I'm superstitious—at least when it comes to making predictions. But there's one message on our answering machine that no one is allowed to erase. Just came in a week ago. Dirk Sutro? Max Lucero? No, not this time.

Here, listen.

"Andy. Hi! It's me, Glory. We won today! I won. It was glory-ous! You *have* to come up here for one of our games, okay? Really, really, I mean it. I reee-ly meeeen it. Oh, wait. *Wait.* Mom! I will. Let *go*! Andy? Sorry, Mom wants to say something. Hold on. Here she is."

"Andy? Hi! It's me, Marlina. Tell your dad— you'll never guess. Tell him I met an old friend of your grandfather's from way back. He's still in the business, and I played him our CD. He loves the songs, my voice, everything. He wants me to record an album. I'm dying! It is so cool. But, listen. His name is Moss Hartman, and when he found out that it was you—the grandson of Gilberto Ramos—playing trumpet behind me, he went la la. He was delirious. Serious. Andy, call me back. He said he'd heard you before and wants you guys, FuChar Skool, to play behind me. Loves the guitar work. Loves the drums. Call us back, okay? We love you. We miss you. We ree-ly, ree-ly, and I meeen reee-ly—"

"Mom, shut *up*! Give me that. Don't hang—"

the fuchar is now in session

Future's Cool with FuChar Skool, Singer

SAN FRANCISCO—Loose Arrow Records, a division of Sony, announced today the signing of female vocalist and former Ocean Beach resident Marlina Martinez and local fusion band FuChar Skool to a three-record contract.

"Her voice has the remarkable range and texture of old-school jazz singers such as Billie Holliday and Big Mama Thornton, while catching the modern urban phrasings of hip-hop and rock," said Minnie Church, A&R rep for Loose Arrow Records.

"FuChar Skool provides Marlina with a golden opportunity to marry her unique vocals with unique musical content," added Church. "We're very excited."

Martinez, 35, is a leading Bay Area vocalist. The band is comprised of trumpet player Andy Gil Ramos, 18; guitarist Tran Loc Tien, 19; and drummer Martín "Lil Lobo" Rojas, 19. FuChar Skool, along with Ms. Martinez, is expected to launch an extensive national tour with the release of their first CD this fall, *The FuChar Is Now in Session.*

—AP Special Report to the OB Rag.

FuChar Skool Rox You

Songs of the FuChar

All Words and Music
© Andy Gil Ramos

when they outlaw freedom, only outlaws will be free

Words and Music © Andy Gil Ramos

"This one, it's kind of rockabilly punk, with the ghosts of Ray Charles and my grandpa walking all through it."

          Am   **Dm**   **Am**

Chorus: Freedom!   Freedom!   Has got to be free

Slow

      When they take it from you, boys,

               C

        they take it from me

    D

And when they outlaw freedom,

              E   **Am**

      only outlaws will be free.

Upbeat, nice and sweet

       Am

I   Take it from a skateboarder,

              down the corridor, songwriter,

              Cross the border, freedom fighter

   Dm

   Boys an' girls, all whirled,

   Baseball, softball, blend 'em all, fusion swirl.

Am

Profused, confused, blown fuse, time to choose,

   E   **Am**

To fight back, baby, you got nothin' to lose.

Chorus: ('Cept) Freedom! Freedom! Got to free yourself,

     Think you're free, but you're livin' in a cell,

     If freedom's got strings, you better call it

     something else.

Trumpet solo

II   Take it from a softball, over the wall,

    Tower 7, footprint fall

    Son and daughter, cannon fodder, don't ask

        why, mean, why bodder?

    Walk in a fog, don't dialog, or they'll leash

        and lash you like a dog.

    Day by day, liber-tay is chipped an' stripped

        an' ripped away

    Till there's no one left free to say

    (We want our) Freedom! Freedom!

        An' it better be free

    When they take it from you, dawg,

        they take it from me

    And when they outlaw freedom

        only outlaws will be free.

III   Take it from a Mexican, American,
Indian, born-again,
      Tao and Zen!
Free dem boyz, free dem grrlz!
College, knowledge, pass the test, look yer best
Go, baby, go, y'awn the road to suck-cess.

Chorus: (But it ain't) Freedom! Freedom!
Don't you take it from me.
Allah God's chillun, brudda, got to see
When they outlaw freedom,
only outlaws will be free.
(Repeat last line)

Trumpet, guitar, and drums improv
(Repeat final chorus)

arm's reach away

Words and Music © Andy Gil Ramos

"Slow down, you got to feel it."

Trumpet solo intro

    A   D   A

Saw a star last night just an arm's reach away.

              C   D   A

Saw a star burn bright just an arm's reach away

              C   D   F   A

Saw a fool reach out, but then I turned away.

Saw a fool last night try an' touch a star
Saw a fool by the lamppost reach out
            to clutch a star
Saw a fool last night takin' down his guitar.

What do you do when your heart's
            an arm's reach away?
What do you do when your dreams're
            walkin' away?
What happens when your best laid plans've
            all gone stray?

Saw a friend last night sittin' just an
            arm's reach away.
Watched a friend last night, watched her arms
            reach my way.

Words spun my head, but I could not find
the ones to say.

Heard a voice last night tell me he's goin' away.
Heard a voice last night say,
"I've said all I need to say."
Said, "Now you crazy dreamers,
now it's time to play."

FUNdaMENTAL FUsioN

Words and Music © Andy Gil Ramos

"Straight ahead, man. Don't wait for me."

Party beat, uptempo

   G   C
Earth, wind, fire, life's illusions
   G   D
Take 'em to the water, boys, and infuse 'em.
      G G7   C A C D G
That's fun. Funda-mental. That's fusion.

Spoken: [Fusion? Fusion!]

Trumpet and guitar improv, call and response

     C   F   C F
Chorus: It begins and ends with F-U-N.
     C   F   G   G7
     Say it with me, I'll say it again. [Fusion!]
     C   F   C F C F
     Begins and ends with F-U-N.
        G
     It's built in!

Spoken: [That's my spin.]

Daytime moonlight's no illusion.
Want some fries with that delusion?
Moon, sun, hey, shorty, that's fusion.

Trumpet and drums improv, call and response

Spoken: [Fusion? Fusion!]

Chorus: Begins and ends with F-U-N.
I'll say it again, hear it, my friend. [Fusion!]
Begins and ends with F-U-N.
I'll say it again.
It's built in!

Spoken: [Bulletin!]

degrees of love
Words and Music © Andy Gil Ramos

*"This one's calypso, basically. But, you know, sing it
like a jolly moon. It's definitely dancehall. Good spirit,
all shaka. The Latin jazz part's the trumpet solo, and the
Latin beat comes in again at the fade-out."*

<pre>
         G   C   G
Have you heard about the degrees of love?
                             D
I never got 'em, cuz I never got enough
G   C   G
Now I see 'em an' they're step-by-step rough
                         D   G
But you gotta walk 'em, the degrees of love.
</pre>

Maybe she was not, maybe she was,
Maybe she does not, maybe she does.
All depends on the fire in her blood,
An' that depends upon the degrees of love.

I never knew the degrees of love,
But now I know no doubt,
          there's degrees of love.
Takes a little bit of push and a little bit of shove,
To break on through the degrees of love.

Trumpet solo improv.

Maybe she was not, maybe she was,
Maybe she does not, maybe she does.
All depends on the fire in your blood,
When you ollie up the degrees of love.
When you tolly up the degrees of love.
When you dolly up the degrees of love.
When you jolly up the degrees of love.
When you molly up the degrees of love.
When you lollipop the degrees of love.

Everywhere you go, it's degrees of love,
Everyone you know, it's degrees of love.
Ay, yi, yi, yi, yi, the degrees of love!
Ay, yi, yi, yi, yi, the degrees of love!
Fade-out: I am astounded by degrees of love
I am surrounded by degrees of love.
I am confounded by degrees of love
I'm slippin' an' slidin' in de greeze of love.

birdwing blues

Words and Music © Andy Gil Ramos

"Well, this one still hurts. But it's just, you know,
straight trad twelve-bar blues with a bad-boy beat."

E
I went down to the pier, boys,
       took my guitar along.
A
Took my guitar to the pier, boys,
                   E
       gonna write me a song.
B7
Rolled down to the birdwing,
          A   G   E
       an' everybody there was gone.

I sat up on the rail, boys,
       played out into the night.
I heft up on the rail, tried to
       write a song that night.
But every sound that did come out,
       did not come out soundin' right.

Robert Johnson, Robert Johnson,
       where you been so long?

Robert Johnson, Robert Johnson,
        where you been so long?
Did I see you on the birdwing,
        when everyone there was gone?

I was lookin' to the stars,
        but I could not find the moon.
I jump down to the crossway,
        but I could not find the moon.
Then a man come walkin' by,
        said my guitar was not a-tune.

Standin' on the birdwing,
        it was sometime in June.
Standin' on the crossroads,
        on a cold, dark night in June.
He wore a black suit and a red tie,
        and a hat to block the moon.

He did not take a penny, did not take a dime.
Did not take a nickel, did not take one dime.
Only took my ol' six-string an' all my good
        and happy times.
Then he asked me with a grin, "Boy?
        Why your music sound so fine?"

that night down by the river

Words and Music © Andy Gil Ramos

*"Okay, here I am, I'm in the street, Newport, just skating
along, totally ensconced in this Bob Marley CD. I think the
track was 'Buffalo Soldier.' And across the street, here
comes this really cute chick walking up, you know, out of
the corner of my eye? And it turns out to be Glory, which
I only realize after she waves. But the light changes, and
I'm late anyway, so I just wave back and head to practice.
But then this whole song just kind of grew out of that
one fine moment."*

G   Em

I was down, down, movin' on downtown,

G   D G

Me an' Bob Marley was a-rockin' away.

         Em

I was down, down, idlin' at a stoplight,

G   D G

when I seen a woman lookin' my way.

      D G

Yeah, I seen a woman lookin' my way.

D   C G

And, oh, whoa, she waved an' she hollered.

D   C G

Oh, B! Now, she done a little dance.

<pre>
       D   C   G
And, oh, Bobby, well, it's been such a long time
                   D   G
since I seen a woman take that kinda chance,
                   D   G
since I seen a woman take that kinda chance.

             D   C   G
'Cuz, y'know, I'm a lover an' I sure can deliver.
D   C
Boys, you shoulda seen me
                                    G
          on that night down by the river.
          D
It was me and a lovin' lady
                    C   G
          an' we sent the town a-shiver.
</pre>

We was down, down, movin' on downtown,
Me an' Bob Marley was a-rockin' away.
We was down, down passin'
          Willie's Shoe Shine,
When she said, oh, yeah, yeah, later in the day.
When she said, oh, yeah, yeah, later in the day.
And, oh, whoa, she said that night
          she'd be there.
Oh, B! Then she done a little dance.
And, oh, Bobby, well, it's been such a long time

since I seen a woman take that kinda chance,
since I seen a woman take that kinda chance.

'Cuz, you know, I'm a lover an' I sure can deliver.
Boys, you shoulda seen me on that night
                    down by the river.
It was me and a lovin' lady
                    an' we sent the town a-shiver.

We was down, down, movin' on downtown,
Me an' Bob Marley was a-rockin' away.
We was down, down, movin' on downtown,
Me an' Bob Marley was a-shockin' away.
Me an' Bob Marley was a-flockin' away.
Me an' Bob Marley shaka-shakin' away.
I say, me an' Bob Marley was a-rockin' away.

say me, war you in on niss?

Words and Music © Andy Gil Ramos

"Reggae, you know, all the way. Rock steady. Sublime."

Run through the chorus once as instrumental intro

    G   Em G
First I ask Kayla,

                  D G
"Didja know about the stranjah?"

    G   Em G
I say, "You get one big kiss,

                D G
if you say me who war in on niss."

(She say,)
G   Em D
"How can we
G Em D
talk to you
G   Em   D
'bout a conversation
      C   E7 G
we never did do?"

Chorus:

[*Everyone sings.*]

> **G   D**
> "How can we
> **G   D**
> talk to you
> **G   D**
> 'bout a conversation
> **G   Em   A   G**
> we never did do?"
>
> I walk on to Glory,
> ask her for the story.
> Say, "You certain get one hug an' kiss,
> if you say me who war in on niss.
> So come on, go rock steady."
> She say, "Been there an' back already."
> ("I mean,)
> how can we
> talk to you
> 'bout a conversation
> we never did do?"

(Repeat chorus. Everyone sings.)

> I ask Lil Lobo
> "Did you ever talka HoJo?"
> He say, "Jes one minute, Moe,
> now you are free to go."

("Say,)
how can we
talk to you
'bout a conversation
we never did do?"

(Repeat chorus. Everyone sings.)

"Now," I say, "Tran the Man,
please, tell to me what you can."
He say, "You got to understand,
you put me in one jam-jam."

(He say,)
"How can we
talk to you
'bout a conversation
we never did do?"

(Repeat chorus. Everyone sings.)

Dakota, she one sly fox,
if anyone talk, she talks.
I ask her for da true trute,
She say, "Why don' you talka Doctor Root?"

("Becuz,)
how can we
talk to you
'bout a conversation
we never did do?"

(Repeat chorus. Everyone sings.)

> Every friend on my list
> I ask 'em, "War you in on niss?"
> They all looka me wit eyeballs
> crawlin' up and down the walls.
>
> (Sayin',)
> "How can we
> talk to you
> 'bout a conversation
> we never did do?"

(Repeat chorus. Everyone sings.)

> I say, okay, that's cool.